TUCKER

CONTEMPORARY WESTERN

THE BURNETT BRIDES
BOOK SEVEN

SYLVIA MCDANIEL

VIRTUAL BOOKSELLER

The Bodyguard, The Actress, and the Matchmaking Ghost

Billionaire Tucker Burnett keeps his international security business and personal life separate even when he's protecting the world's most beautiful women. When his client is almost killed, he takes her to the only place he knows she'll be safe – his family's ranch – and hopes his ancestral ghost behaves herself.

Kendra Woods is the biggest star in Hollywood, but she's got a secret. Someone wants her dead. When her handsome bodyguard whisks her away to the boonies, she's more than a little miffed. Especially, when he gives her exactly what she needs.

The Burnett ghost insists that Kendra can have the family she's always longed for with the man who would lay down his life for her. But can she give up the life of luxury and fame to be a rancher's wife?

Does their love have a ghost of a chance?

CHAPTER 1

*T*ucker Burnett stared across his desk at his favorite employee at Burnett Security. Damn, he had to fire him and he hated that.

But Tucker was a rule follower and if you broke a rule, you suffered the consequences.

Quinn had broken a very important rule. One that everyone in the company knew you'd receive your walking papers for committing.

In some ways, Tucker felt like their Aunt Rose trying to rein in his brother Tanner and now wife, Emily, which caused Aunt Rose more problems than it had been worth. He hoped it wasn't the same for him.

At least he didn't have a video of them having sex in the kitchen.

But losing his best employee would make his life harder. A good employee was difficult to find, and over the years, he'd built a good team. Right now, he trusted his men. Until he learned what his best guy had done.

"Look, boss, I know what you're going to say. But hear me out."

Oh, he'd hear him out, all right, and then walk him right out the door. Lives could have been lost. He'd put the entire operation at risk. Not to mention they had lost the account. A very lucrative account.

"You broke the rules. How can our clients depend on us if we don't follow our own regulations? Not to mention that you endangered the client and yourself. Your emotions got involved and when that happens you don't make rational decisions. Especially when your dick is inside a beautiful woman."

The man shifted uncomfortably in his chair staring at him. "You're right. But nothing happened. I didn't plan on falling in love with the hottest model in the world. In fact, I ran away from those feelings. I refused to acknowledge them until..."

Tucker felt his insides tighten. "Until what?"

"Until she asked me to spend the night in her bedroom. She was scared. I slept in there for five nights sitting upright in a chair, then one night after the stalker tried to attack her, I caved. When she threw her arms around me and pressed her sweet body against mine, it was over."

This kind of disobedience he had to squash right now. If he let Quinn get away with having sex with the client, then the others would begin to think of him as soft. And Tucker was anything but soft.

In fact, he was known to his employees for being a hard-ass. And that's the way he liked it.

"And what was this client known for?"

The man sighed and licked his lips nervously. "Sex parties. Do you know how many of those damn events I had to stand there and watch? Disgusting."

A shudder went through Tucker. That right there was enough to turn him completely off sleeping with the client.

"No, but I would think it would make you reconsider where you're going to put your dick."

The man shook his head. "I tried. I don't like sharing a woman with anyone. But those damn models would come up to me and rub all over me. They would tempt and tease me and then Sasha…"

Before Tucker accepted the job, he knew it would be a difficult assignment, so he'd given it to his strongest man. The person he trusted to keep his dick in his pants and he'd failed. Failed miserably.

In some ways, this was his own fault for taking on this client. It was for the best that she had fired them.

"Did you ever think that the stalker might have paid the models to tempt you, so he could slip away with Sasha? While they were rubbing on you, he was pursuing our client."

The man sighed. "I didn't sleep with anyone but Sasha. No one. I stood like a soldier with a stiffee at those ridiculous parties. They're sick and twisted, man. Nothing that I ever want to see again."

Tucker sighed and leaned back in his chair. He had no choice. No one slept with the client. No one. Not even when you were comforting them.

Not even when the client's friends were tempting you to join them.

Not even when the client was a beautiful model who tempted you with her body. Never. Just never.

Shaking his head he stared at his employee, a big burly guy with bulging biceps. "This assignment was given to you because I believed in you the most. We talked about how the stalker was probably at one of these wild parties she liked to attend. That he was probably a rejected lover. And yet you failed to keep your head out of your ass."

The man sighed and shook his head. "No, not at the parties. Never at the parties. Just with Sasha at her home."

Why he thought that made it better, Tucker didn't know.

"This is strictly against our standard operating practice. I have no choice but to fire you."

The man put his face in his hands. "I know. You're right. When you called me in, today, I thought I would be fired. And you proved me right. I was wrong and I hoped when I admitted my mistake, you would give me a pass this time. After what's gone down, I can promise you it would never happen again."

This sucked. But the rules were there for a reason. A good reason.

"For your sake, I hope she's stopped attending these wild parties and you're happy," Tucker said. "Because she just cost you your job."

The man leaned back in his chair. "Hell, she dumped me. It was nothing more than a one-night stand. *We're not compatible* is what she told me. I'm not the rich playboys she likes to hang with. I'm a working-class guy. She wanted a rich leading man or another supermodel."

Tucker sighed. He'd lost his best man because of this selfish bitch. "Well, if it makes you feel any better, she fired us this morning. Breach of contract for getting sexually involved. This is why I insist no sexual involvement."

The man's eyes widened and he clenched his fist. "She came on to me. She begged me to go to bed with her. To hold her and then she got naked."

Some women liked to tempt a man as far as they could. And many men took the bait and then were sucker punched. Quinn had just been sucker punched.

"I need your badge, your revolver, and the company car you drove," Tucker said. "I'll give you two weeks' severance pay."

Quinn sighed and slowly stood. "This job is tough. Especially tough when a sexy woman is tempting you. It was a fun job and I must say she was good. Next time, you protect a beautiful, sexy woman who keeps coming on to you, let's see how well you stand up against the constant temptation. The manipulation."

Staring at Quinn, Tucker knew he'd made his own mistake in

giving him the job. Maybe Tucker should have taken on the job. Hell, he was a damn eunuch, only he still had his balls.

"Get out," Tucker said, "before I take away your two weeks' severance pay."

The man smiled. "I'm going. But when was the last time you were with a woman? I bet you wouldn't hold out for long. You'll crater, just like I did. And when you do, think of me."

The man turned and walked out the door.

With a sigh, Tucker leaned back in his chair. It had been years since he'd been with a woman. Years. But he was building a business and there was no time for women. And no, he was not into one-night stands, even though he'd convinced his brother Tanner.

In today's world, people needed protection from criminal elements. He'd learned that the hard way. Only an inch had separated him from death. And now he lived his life protecting others.

CHAPTER 2

*K*endra Woods had worked hard to reach the top.
As a child, she'd sung in the church choir and it
was there she learned people enjoyed hearing her sing. After her
fifth number-one hit, she'd auditioned for a movie and gotten the
part. Now she spent her time between movies, holding concerts
or singing in Las Vegas.

She'd gone from being a poor girl barely surviving to one of
the richest performers in Hollywood. And she liked her life.
Actually, she loved her life and performing.

It was her passion. The poor girl from Mississippi no longer
had to worry where her next meal was coming from or whether
her father would come home drunk. She'd escaped the life of
poverty and she never planned on returning.

Tonight, she was performing in the Hollywood Bowl with a
full orchestra and the tickets had been sold out for months. The
practice sessions had gone great and she couldn't wait to perform
tonight.

Opening the door to her dressing room, she halted mid step
at the sight of an envelope lying on the floor. Her heart slammed

into her chest and she stared at the paper knowing there would be no fingerprints on the envelope.

She was the target of some sick pervert. Like hot lava, anger flooded her veins. She'd worked hard to make it to the top. Some asshole was not going to scare her. After all, working in Hollywood was a fight to survive and she was a prizefighter.

Get in the ring with her and you would walk away bloodied. This pervert needed his ass kicked. And oh how she longed to bloody his nose.

Grabbing her cell phone out of her purse, she called her agent.

"There's another one," she said, staring at the paper on the floor, wishing she could just set it on fire.

"Don't open it. I'm on my way," Anthony said. "Have you called the police?"

"No, why would I? *Miss Woods, there are no fingerprints. Nothing to connect this back to the person who placed it here,*" she said in a mocking tone that had been repeated to her twice now. "What's the point? This asshole is going to get away with it until I take matters into my own hands."

"Kendra, don't do anything. I'm almost there," he said.

"Hurry, makeup is due to arrive any moment."

With a click, she ended the conversation and began to dress not bothering to touch the envelope in the middle of the floor, tempted to kick it out of her way. But that would be touching it.

Knowing the police would arrive with Anthony, she pulled on the tight silver dress that had a thousand or more sequins. The floor-length gown fit her curves, and as soon as her stylists arrived, they would have her looking stunning.

Not bad for a girl from the muddy backwaters. Not bad for a girl who came from a family who nearly starved to death waiting on their drunken father to bring home groceries. Not bad for a girl who graduated high school and worked her way up the charts.

Now they were all gone but her sister Nancy, who held a

steady job at the local hospital as the head of ICU. They had both been determined to get out of the bad situation they were living in, and each had chosen a direct path to the life they wanted.

Nancy was married with two small children that Kendra adored. She hoped to see her before she started her next movie. She needed to squeeze those babies and remind them that she loved them.

They were her only family and she wished they lived closer.

A knock on the door sounded and Anthony strolled in along with the L.A. police.

"It's there on the floor," she said. "I didn't touch it."

A detective wearing plain clothes and latex gloves crouched and picked it up and started to put it in an evidence bag.

"Oh no," Kendra said, looking at him. "Open it. I want to know what it says before you take it."

Living in the back woods, you quickly learned not to trust the law officials. And while she was certain this man was a good policeman, she wasn't taking a chance. She insisted they read the note to her.

He frowned and then gently opened the envelope.

Once again, she saw the letters cut from a magazine and formed into a sentence.

The policeman read the note. "This is your third and final warning. Retire or die."

She started laughing. "I'm only twenty-six and this jerk wants me to retire? Hell, I just got started with my career. I plan on being around for a long time. So he can take his social security message and hang himself."

The cops looked uneasy at her and Anthony reached out and rubbed her arm. This had started two weeks ago right after she learned she'd received the lead role in the new movie she auditioned for. But she didn't think this had anything to do with the movie. How could it?

"Where are hair and makeup? I'm going on stage in forty-five minutes."

"We kept them out," the officer said.

"Well, send them in. I have a show to perform," she told the man, slipping her heels on. They were silver to match her dress with three-inch stilettos that would have her feet screaming by the end of the show.

Anthony touched her and turned her to face him. "Maybe you should reconsider going on tonight. We don't know if there is some looney out in the crowd that is going to shoot or hurt you. This is not worth the risk."

Just then the makeup girl came in with her suitcase of colors that would make her beautiful. She motioned for the girl to come around the men.

"Not a chance," she said, sinking into the chair in front of the lighted mirror. "These people paid good money to hear me tonight and I'm going to sing for them."

Anthony sighed and shook his head. "I knew you would say that."

He turned to the L.A. policemen. "Can we have extra security around the arena?"

The two men looked at each other. "Let me check with the chief."

They walked out the door and Kendra began her deep breathing to help her relax before her show. This idiot, whoever he was, was making her more nervous than she'd been at that first rehearsal almost ten years ago.

Screw him. He wasn't going to win.

The makeup artist pulled her unruly auburn hair back and got busy putting on the layers of foundation. It was a process she'd grown accustomed to. One that when the girl finished, she would look like a cover model.

"Kendra, if you refuse to cancel the show tonight, at least let me call and hire a security company. I know a good one. Tucker Burnett is the best in the business."

A security company that would follow her around worse than the crazy fans who waited outside the door of the venue, outside her home, or followed her car. One more person pursuing her. Just no.

Privacy was a wonderful thing that she'd never considered losing until fame found her. Now she craved it more than anything.

"No," she said firmly. "All he's sent are letters. Sooner or later, I'm going to catch him at it, and when I do, he'll be arrested."

The L.A. police came back into the room. She could see from their faces they weren't happy with the news they'd received.

"Since this was not arranged in advance, we're not able to get authorization for tonight."

Taking a deep breath, she smiled at the men, recognizing they were only doing their jobs. "Thank you. I appreciate what you've done here tonight. Let me know if you find any fingerprints on the envelope."

They smiled and looked relieved she had not gone all diva on them. But what could she expect? They were just part of the system.

"Thank you, ma'am," one of the two men said.

"Would you like an autograph as a personal thank you?"

"Yes, please," they both replied.

"Could you make mine out to my wife?" the youngest officer said. "She's expecting our first born and she'll be so thrilled."

She smiled at the man and quickly picked up a program and signed it. "Thank you for your help and congratulations, Officer."

A tinge of jealousy filled her. Oh, to be married and having a family. But with her lifestyle, it just wasn't possible to find a man who wanted to follow her from city to city watching her perform. Or now from a movie set. No man liked being called

Mr. Woods, and over the years, she'd given up dating and relationships. But a family was something she secretly longed for.

It was the reason she spoiled her nieces.

"Make mine out to me. Officer John Daly," he said. "I like your movies the best."

"Oh, which one," she asked.

"The one where you were the romance writer struggling to survive," he said, laughing. "That was pretty funny."

"I'm glad I made you happy," she told the man and quickly signed his program before she handed it to him. "Thank you, gentlemen. I hope we don't have to call you again."

"Goodnight, ma'am," they both said and walked out the door.

The makeup artist lined her eyes and the hairdresser had arrived and was combing out and putting her hair up in a twist.

Anthony stood off to the side watching. "We're running late."

"Almost done," the makeup artist said.

"Finished," the hairdresser said spraying her strands.

No time for her usual relaxation meditation before she went on stage. Instead, she channeled all the anger she felt toward this jerk that was hell-bent on scaring her into retirement. She refused to let him win.

The makeup artist applied lipstick to her mouth.

"All done," she said.

"Come on," Anthony said, helping her rise from the chair. "Time to go."

At the door, she stopped and turned back to the women who had worked on her. "Thank you, ladies. I look lovely as always because of you."

These people helped make her into a star and she always made certain that she thanked them and even threw in a little extra well-deserved cash.

They smiled. "You're welcome. Have a good show."

She grinned and let Anthony lead her out the door.

"If I yell at you to drop, you do so immediately," he said. "I'm going to be watching the crowd."

"I'll be fine," she said as the technicians wired her up. "Besides, do you really believe I could drop in this dress?"

Anthony shook his head and smiled. "It fits well."

When they reached the stage, she glanced at the orchestra leader and the director. He gave her the thumbs up and the music began to play. Taking a deep breath, she smiled as pleasure filled her and opened her mouth to vocalize a long, deep rumble.

The audience screamed as she walked out on stage. For the next forty minutes, she did her best to give them the performance they had come to see. She belted out tune after tune and kicked up her heels and even did a little dance.

The audience loved it.

When she stopped for a breath. She smiled at them. "Sorry, that's my backwoods Mississippi jig coming out."

Three more songs and she would be finished. The car would be waiting to whisk her away and take her home.

She always saved her favorite song for last, and when she started to sing the sweet melody, the crowd went crazy. When she reached the chorus, she moved closer to the edge of the stage. "Sing the lyrics with me."

A ripping sound resounded behind her as a light bar crashed onto the stage where she had been just a moment ago.

The electricity popped and glass rolled across the stage.

Stunned, she stared at the damage.

Was that on purpose? Had the perpetrator tried to kill her?

The band stopped and she glanced out at the audience.

"Are you guys okay?" she asked.

They were speechless for a moment. Then finally someone yelled, "Yes."

"I'm all right. Kind of too close for comfort, but I'm fine."

She turned to the orchestra. "Are you guys all right?"

They nodded, but she could see that many of them were shaken.

"Then let's take it home," she said and the leader lifted his wand. Once again, she began to sing, but her knees were shaking, and inside, she was vibrating with nerves. This had turned into a war, and he'd just fired the first shot. But she wasn't giving up.

Oh, hell no, this made her madder. You didn't ruin her performance in front of an audience. Now she just felt anger.

She leaned back and belted out the last few notes of the song. At the end, she blew the audience a kiss and walked off the stage.

When she reached Anthony, she could see he was white as a ghost.

"Call that fucking security company. This ass is not going to win."

CHAPTER 3

*T*ucker had his iPad with him as he walked around Kendra Woods's mansion in Beverly Hills. Late last night, her agent, Anthony Emanuel, had called him in a panic.

"I need you," he said. "We've had three letters telling her to retire, and last night at her concert, a light bar fell and almost hit her."

"Saw it on the news," Tucker told him. "Pretty damn scary."

"Yes, and she's so stubborn, she refuses to cancel her concerts. Plus, we're supposed to start a movie in two months. This has got to end before then."

"You know my requirements. A full security evaluation before I take on any job."

It did no good to protect someone if their property was not secure. You could follow them around, but once they arrived home, they became targets.

"What time can you meet us at the house?"

"How about nine a.m.," Tucker said. "I'll bring my security detail to help me go over the house and property."

"Just get here as soon as you can," Anthony said. "I'm spending the night with her instead of going home to my family. I think tonight really shook her up."

Many times, his clients thought they were simply being harassed by an unhappy fan until that person got too close to them. This sounded even more dangerous. How had they made the equipment fail without anyone knowing they were there?

This morning, Tucker had arrived before nine o'clock to check out how safe and secure her mansion was and what would be needed before he took her on as a client.

Judd, one of his best men, checked the electrical connections and phone lines, and verified the cameras situated around the house. Ben analyzed the property to see how someone could get in.

Tucker drew a diagram of the layout of the grounds. When he walked inside the home, Anthony met him at the door.

"And?"

"I need to go through the house and diagram the layout," he said. "Then after everyone reports in, we'll sit down and give you our evaluation."

The smell of coffee hung in the air and he longed for a cup. But that was impossible. He was working.

"Are you planning on selling pictures of my clothes to the paparazzi?" a cool feminine voice said behind him.

He whirled around and saw the most stunning woman he'd ever laid eyes on. Auburn hair hung down past her shoulders and stunning eyes the color of bluebonnets in Texas gazed at him. Damn, she was gorgeous.

"Ma'am, the paparazzi dislike me immensely, so no, I won't be selling them pictures of anything. Not even your stalker when I catch him."

She lifted the coffee cup to her lips and regarded him, her blue eyes suspicious. "Anthony, go with him."

A client who distrusted him. Great. Maybe this wasn't a job he wanted after all. His gut instinct told him to turn this one down after the model's job. Look how that turned out, and he'd ignored his gut instincts on that one.

As they walked up the stairs, Tucker glanced back at Anthony. "Is she always this warm and friendly with the help?"

He laughed. "She's had a really rough couple of days. But no, one thing about Kendra is that she's always direct."

"Oh, good. A diva," he said. "My favorite kind of client."

Anthony laughed. "No, she's not a diva, by any means. She's all business. Snappy and direct and no bullshit. Don't even think about lying to her or she will call you out. She's a southern girl who doesn't take shit from anyone."

At least that sounded better. But still, most of the stars he interacted with were big whiny bitches who didn't like his suggestions on keeping them safe until they got into trouble. Then they wailed and cried and tried to blame him for their troubles.

"Good to know," he said.

For the next thirty minutes, he walked the house, sketching a diagram of each window, each door, and checking the locks and even the blinds in each room. In addition, he took pictures out the windows so he knew the vulnerability points.

This house was not secure and it was a wonder she hadn't had pictures taken by the paparazzi of her inside the house. All they had to do was climb the tree outside her lot and they could see straight into the upstairs.

A helicopter flying over could take pictures of her swimming pool, the cabana house, and even the cars in the drive. Why stars didn't consult him before they purchased a mansion, he didn't know. But afterward, they came to him and said *make it secure.*

Sometimes that just wasn't possible.

After the last room, he glanced at Anthony. "I'm done. Let's go find the other men."

His assistants were standing outside the front door leaning up against his car.

"Come in," he said to the men. "It's time to talk to the client."

They walked inside and gazed around at the tall ceilings, the beautiful tile floors, and the huge chandelier hanging above them.

"Nice," Judd said. "Really nice."

Anthony motioned for them to follow him.

"Is there a place we can sit and talk?" he asked Anthony.

"Let's go in the kitchen. I'll get Kendra," he said.

They walked into an immense kitchen with a big family room off to the side showcasing a rock fireplace taking up one wall. Large windows looked out over the sparkling water of the pool.

A small table sat by the windows in the kitchen where they sat waiting for Kendra.

Stars always felt like their time was important, but yours they couldn't care less about. It was a frustrating part of the job.

After ten minutes, she came down the stairs, with the phone in her hand.

"I've got to go. Really, I'm fine. No, I'm not going to come out there and endanger you and the kids. That would be crazy."

She held the phone to her ear.

"No, they would know where I'm at. I've got one more concert and then I'm done until after my next movie. And no, I'm not going to let this fool scare me into hiding."

Walking into the kitchen, she stood at the table. "Look, the security team is waiting on me. I've got to go. Love you too."

As soon as she hung up, she glanced around the group. "Sorry, that was my sister wanting me to return to Mississippi. Not happening."

Tucker gazed at this woman and wondered how she had become a star. Where had she gotten her training and who taught her to sing so beautifully? Because she had a voice that left you wanting more.

Anthony shook his head. "Tell us what you found."

Tucker glanced at his men. They had done this plenty of times. Ben gave his report first, telling of at least five places the fence around the home was weakened and could be easily breached. Then Judd gave his report and told how the phone lines could be very easily cut, shutting down the security system. The electrical box was better but still not great. The cameras around the house did not cover the utilities.

Kendra glanced at the two men. "Is there anything you can tell me that would make me feel safe? Right now, I'm thinking I'm a sitting star just waiting for her stalker to break in."

"Yes, ma'am, you are," Judd said. "Your security system is from the nineties and needs to be updated."

Leaning back in the chair, she shook her head and looked at Tucker, and for the first time ever, he went blank. All that red hair and her gorgeous eyes drew him in, and for a second, he forgot what he was doing. Then he remembered Quinn's warning.

Oh hell, no.

"What good news do you have for me?"

A smile crossed his face. "Well, the paparazzi can't see into your bedroom, so that's a good thing. You have four doors coming into the house and none of them have a camera or anything to let you know the door has been opened. Your cameras are in places that do not cover the entire house. The windows do not have alarms on them. So anyone can break into the house pretty easy."

Shaking her head, she glared at him. "Thank you for making me feel like I need to move to a hotel."

Long ago, he'd learned never to respond, but rather to sit and let the client think about their exposure. And he noted her eyes were wide as she looked about the room. "I've always loved this house. Maybe I should move."

"Or maybe you should let us bring it up to standard," Tucker said.

A frown appeared between her eyes. "But I thought you would just protect me when we leave the house?"

This is what they always thought.

"We will, but what good does it do for us to protect you when you're out and about, but leave you vulnerable here at home? Most attacks occur at home."

She bit her full lip and he looked away. The woman was gorgeous, smart, and direct. Everything he admired in a woman, and yet there was also a sense of vulnerability about her that he had the most incessant urge to protect.

"How much is your service to protect me and also upgrade the security at my home going to cost?"

"A rough estimate is one hundred thousand dollars," he said, knowing she would balk at his price, but she needed a full upgrade. Right now, her situation was critical.

"Are you out of your flipping mind?"

"That's twenty-four-hour security for ninety days. A complete upgrade on the security in your home and one of my men driving you everywhere you want to go. Someone from Burnett security will be by your side at all times."

Licking her lips, she shook her head. "That's a lot of money. What do other security details cost?"

They always wanted their protection at a low cost and Tucker wasn't cheap. As the best in the business, she would be well protected.

"Ma'am, I'm worth a lot of money. Your current security system can be breached easily."

Anthony leaned toward her. "Tucker is the best."

Standing, Kendra frowned at him. "Just remember if I die, I will come back and haunt you." Her voice had a frustrated angry tone. "Do the upgrades."

Tucker couldn't keep the grin from his face. "I recognize that tone. You mean *fuck you and your company*."

Anthony gasped and snickered all at the same time. His employees smiled but looked away.

She smiled coolly at him. "Yes, that's exactly what it means.

This damn stalker is costing me a lot of green. Like I said, if I die, I'll haunt you. I hope you're worth every penny."

"I am," Tucker said with a smile. "Ma'am, I'm not going to let you die. The world would never forgive me."

"And drop the damn ma'am stuff. I'm not your grandmother."

"No, you're not," he said with a laugh, recalling that his grandmother *was* the one who haunted him. "My secretary will send over the contracts. As soon as everything is signed, we'll get started right away. One of my men will be staying the night here. You'll have twenty-four-hour security. Do you have a place for them to sleep?"

"Yes, the cabana," she said.

That wasn't exactly where he wanted his men. He would rather someone stayed in the house, but for now, he wouldn't argue with her. When the time came, she would agree to let them stay inside.

Already, he could tell this was going to be a very detailed operation.

With a sigh, she turned to walk away. "Let's hope we catch this jerk soon."

Tucker watched her leave, her hips swaying in the tight pants she wore as she hurried up the stairs. There was an office up there and he watched as she walked inside.

Gazing at her, he thought of Quinn. Had the man's wishes come true? Was he now protecting a beautiful woman that was a temptation to just look at?

CHAPTER 4

*K*endra felt like she had a shadow following her every move. Sometimes it was even hard to sneak off to the bathroom by herself. It seemed like men were everywhere in her home. There were cameras installed all over the house and being completely clothed at all times was important.

If she ran around half naked, these men would know. Thank goodness she'd been raised by a very conservative mother who didn't allow nudity in the house.

Nothing in her home went unnoticed and she waited for the pictures to show up in the tabloids. The lure of money was too great for even the best men and the tabloids were rich.

Just one photo was worth hundreds of thousands of dollars. Men working security would find that kind of cash a temptation they could not resist. One of her previous housekeepers had sent them a photo of her Grammy Awards gown. The dress made it into the newspapers before she had a chance to wear it. And the housekeeper was now working at a motel down on Hollywood Boulevard.

Hence, her distrustful nature.

For the last two weeks, Tucker had stationed himself outside in her cabana house. He was there twenty-four-seven. Pure hunky all male, he was sleeping, eating, and even showering out there until they caught her stalker.

And all that male hunkiness was hard to ignore. Years ago, she'd realized that her star power and money were something most men could not handle. It intimidated them, and she'd given up on finding someone to spend her life with.

The last serious man had left before she turned twenty, and since then, she occasionally went out but kept things simple. Three dates and they were gone.

But staring at the head of her security detail was a welcome respite in her otherwise dull sexual life. All those toned muscles, those big green eyes, and dark hair that she wanted to run her hands through. Oh yes, she was definitely attracted to Tucker.

Only he didn't seem intimidated by her. In fact, he seemed immune to her star power. Of course, the man had worked with a lot of celebrities. For a couple weeks, his team had roamed her house freely, even locking up at night. Each man seemed to be assigned an area with Tucker in charge in the cabana house.

One man sat in the laundry room watching the cameras on a large monitor that had every angle of her home showing at once. She couldn't even scratch her ass without someone knowing about it.

All because some asshole made her his target.

When she left the house, there was a security detail in front and behind her car. If she raised a window in the house, it triggered a silent alarm that sent men running to her.

They even had her wearing a small tracking device. They knew where she was every moment of the day and it was growing damn old. She wanted her privacy back. She wanted her life back.

And her stalker had gone silent.

Maybe the crashing of the light bar had been an accident. Yet when the investigation team showed her the evidence, it was clear the wires had been cut.

Someone wanted her dead. Someone had almost been successful in getting rid of her. But who?

Today, she'd met with the studio about the upcoming film she would be starting in two months. There was already Oscar buzz. It was being directed by the biggest name in Hollywood and the thought of adding such a prestigious winner to her resume excited her.

Now on her way home, she glanced out the window at the gates. "Wait, let me get the mail."

"I'll get it," her driver said.

She sighed. Tucker had warned her that he didn't want her doing her normal routine. She was beginning to feel like a prisoner in her own home. He had even suggested that she do this meeting via Zoom, but there was no way. So her entourage had followed her to the studios and back.

Nothing had happened. She was beginning to think she'd just spent a hundred thousand dollars for no reason. None.

If the studio learned of her little problem, they might cancel her contract. She really tried to keep the information from getting to the press. So far nothing, but she worried.

The driver got out of the car, shut the door, and locked it. Good grief. He slowly opened her mailbox like he expected a pipe bomb or something to be in there, grabbed the mail, and then came back to the car.

The car in front of them had gone through the gates but stopped and waited. When he opened the door and climbed back in, he was speaking into a mic on his shoulder.

"Yes, sir, she asked me to stop. I understand, sir. It won't happen again," he said.

What the hell? Could she not even grab her own mail?

"Ma'am, Mr. Burnett said no more stopping at the mailbox. One of us will deliver your mail to you."

The man was obsessive about protecting her, and she should feel grateful, but she couldn't get past the irritation. This was her life, and they were interfering, big time.

"Oh good grief," she said. "I think he's a little obsessive."

The man didn't reply but put the car in gear and started up the driveway.

Once the car behind them was through the gate, her driver wouldn't open the door. She tried the door and it wouldn't budge.

"Let me out," she said.

"Not until the gate closes, ma'am," he said.

"You men are so paranoid. I think this security stuff has gone to your brain. Open my door," she insisted.

"Yes, ma'am," the young man said and stepped out of the car and then opened her door.

With a huff, she strode off, the mail in her hand.

Tucker was waiting for her at the door.

"No more mail stops," he said. "It's the perfect opportunity for someone to jump our driver and take off with you."

She stopped and glanced at him. Damn, the man looked handsome standing in front of her, his arms crossed over his chest, his arm muscles bulging. He loomed like a pillar of steel before her with intense emerald eyes that gazed at her and then slid to her lips before returning to her eyes.

If only he was interested in her personally and not in protecting her. Right now, she was at her wits' end.

Enough.

"You guys are driving me crazy. We've not heard from this man in two weeks. Time to back off, cowboy, or I'm going to fire the entire crew."

A slow smile crossed his face, his thick lips so very kissable. "Just doing my job protecting you. If you want to fire us, that's your choice."

It frustrated her that he was right, but still, all this protection left her nervous and sent her anxiety through the roof.

"Let me in the house," she said.

"Not until we get the all-clear," he replied.

Now she couldn't enter her house without it being checked? That was the last straw.

"No," she said, moving to go around him.

His hand reached out and grabbed her arm. "Ma'am, please, my men are going through the house. Once I get the confirmation, you can go in."

A zing of awareness spiraled through her at the strong grip of his fingers on her arm. Had she hired Rambo? That's what it felt like. The man had strength.

"It's my house," she hissed.

"And I'm protecting you," he replied. "I take my job seriously."

How could she fuss at him when he was preventing this stalker from getting to her?

"All clear, sir," a voice said on his microphone.

A smile crossed the man's face. "Let me get the door for you."

He swung open the entrance and stepped to the side. "Have a nice day."

With a grunt, she walked into her home. This couldn't end soon enough.

Kicking off her heels, she walked into the kitchen and poured herself a glass of water. Taking the mail, she went into the living room and plopped onto one of the couches.

Tonight was the big studio celebration for the film they would begin in a couple months. The hairdresser and the makeup artist would arrive around six. She had until then to do what she wanted.

Right now, she just wanted to rest and read through the mail. Most of it was junk that she threw into a pile for her secretary to put through the shredder. There was a card from her nieces telling her they loved her and her heart warmed with love. Her sister had the best life. A husband and two children and a job she loved.

While Kendra loved her job, she realized it made it impossible to have the life she craved. A husband and family. Babies. Nighttime bed stories and school projects. She was missing out on all of that.

Later she would call and thank them for the card.

She picked up the next piece of mail. Insurance. Ugh. The next piece beneath the insurance had her hand freezing. She recognized that handwriting. She'd seen it before.

Oh dear God, no. Why wouldn't he stop?

"Security," she screamed not knowing what else to do.

A man came running into the room.

"What's wrong?"

"This," she said pointing to the letter. "It's from him."

The man spoke into his microphone and instantly, Tucker ran into the room.

"Have you touched it?"

"No, I recognize his handwriting," she said.

"Call the police," Tucker said to his man.

"Is that necessary? Don't you think the paparazzi are going to see a police car driving up my driveway and wonder what's going on? Don't you think the studio is going to get worried and think about canceling my contract if there is a problem?"

Tucker ignored her as he slipped on latex gloves and took the envelope from her lap.

She sighed with relief. Just having it near her made her stomach churn.

"A detective will arrive in a plain car," he said. "I'll make certain of it."

"Oh come on," she said, shaking her head. "Don't you think a plain-clothes detective is recognizable?"

A chuckle came from Tucker. "Probably, but that's the best I can do. I never hide evidence from the police. I never go against the law, and you've already filed several reports with them. They need to see this latest evidence."

With a sigh, she stood and walked out of the room. Yes, she had filed several reports and it had done no good. Nothing had been accomplished. The police in L.A. were slower than the old Sears Christmas catalog arriving. As a child, she remembered waiting for it to come, excited to see all the things her family couldn't afford to buy.

"Kendra, you'll need to be here when they arrive."

"Can a girl get a private bathroom moment?"

"Yes, ma'am," Tucker said, grinning as she walked from the room.

"And stop calling me *ma'am*," she said with a loud hiss.

Going into her bedroom, she glanced about at the room she had decorated to make her happy. She loved this house and this bedroom, but right now, it didn't feel like the safe haven it had always been.

Right now, she was living in an insane asylum.

Going to the closet, she changed from her business attire to a pair of jeans, a T-shirt she loved, and a pair of sneakers. No sense in looking like the star she was. She wanted to fit in when the police arrived. She wanted them to see her as an ordinary citizen.

A scared, frightened ordinary citizen that someone was terrorizing.

With a final glance at her auburn hair, she pulled it back into a ponytail and walked out of the room. She glanced up at the camera aimed at her door. She wanted to flip the operator the bird but that was childish. It wasn't his fault that her stalker had sent another letter.

She wondered what it said, but knew better than to rip open the envelope and read his terse, nasty message.

Going down the stairs, she heard a car door slam.

"They're here," Tucker said, glancing at her.

27

"Let them in," she said. "And watch how the detective acts. I think they believe this is just one big publicity stunt."

Tucker gave her a glance that she couldn't quite read. "Best behavior."

"Always, Tucker, always," she said, putting on her fake smile.

CHAPTER 5

*S*omehow Tucker did not have a good feeling about this interview with the detective. He noticed how on edge Kendra was. Unnerved would be the best description, and yet she was trying to keep it together and act like she was a strong woman.

And she was.

Too damn strong. Sometimes he would just like for her to let him be in charge and keep her safe, but the woman refused to back down.

Seeing her standing on the stairs, looking like an ordinary breathtaking beauty had his defenses ready to take on anyone who tried to harm her.

They would have to go through him first and he would welcome the fight.

Since his company began, he'd been around beautiful women, but he'd never had a reaction to one like Kendra. And it could not continue. As much as he needed to be involved with this job, maybe he should let Judd take over her security and just watch behind the scenes.

That way, he'd be protected from his baser urges. That way he would not do as Quinn had and break his rules.

From two feet away, he smelled the perfume she wore and it was all he could do to keep from reaching for her, his mouth covering her smart, sassy lips and showing her that she was a vulnerable woman.

And that he was a powerful man who found her extremely attractive. Oh, yes, he needed to hand her case over to Judd.

"Good afternoon, Detective," Kendra said, coming down the stairs.

"You received another threat?" the detective asked.

"We haven't opened it. And only the postal employees have handled the letter. It was tucked inside a bunch of mail," Tucker told him.

"It's in the kitchen," she told him. "Would you like something to drink, Detective?"

"No, thank you," the man said, following her into the kitchen/living area. Her home was beautiful.

Gorgeous, but it was in Hollywood. He'd been inside many of the mansions in this area and none of them beat living on the Burnett Ranch. None of them had the peace and serenity he found on his property in Texas.

The detective slipped gloves on and took out his phone and took pictures of the unopened envelope. After he'd taken at least five photographs, he glanced at them.

"It appears to be the same handwriting," he said.

"Yes, I thought so too," she said.

"Have you checked your staff's handwriting? This could be someone who is very close to you," he said.

Her sapphire eyes darkened and cut a glance at Tucker. He could almost hear her mind saying *I told you so*.

What the detective didn't know was that Tucker had already considered that.

"When my company took on this case, we did a thorough

check on all the employees. Including handwriting analysis," Tucker said. "It's not a known staff member."

The detective frowned and took out an evidence bag.

"You are going to open the letter," she said.

"Yes," he told her.

Once he had the envelope inside the evidence bag, he slipped his gloved fingers inside and pulled out the note.

"You should've listened. Strike four, you're dead."

Kendra's face turned white and she stumbled over to the couch and sank down.

"Are you all right?" Tucker asked.

"Yes, I just can't think of why someone would want to kill me. And to hear those words is frightening."

He sat across from her. It was all he could do not to take her trembling hand in his, to offer her comfort. No question, he was getting way too involved. He'd speak to Judd once the detective left.

"You were supposed to protect me," she said, her eyes turning on him in a heated gaze. "I don't feel very safe."

What could he say? So far, their investigation had not stopped this person. It was still early and most breaks came in the first two weeks.

"Are you dead?" It was a sarcastic remark and he regretted it almost as soon as he said it.

"No, but I don't feel safe either," she replied.

"Ma'am, we're not going to let anything happen to you," he promised her.

Her eyes narrowed and he could tell that his words had not made her feel better. In fact, she almost appeared angry.

"Would you please stop with the southern drawl? I'm not a ma'am. I'm scared shitless and your sweet-talking voice is not going to calm me down. Someone wants to kill me. As in no heartbeat, no pulse, no longer a part of this world."

It was the first time Tucker had seen her truly frightened and knew she was finally beginning to realize that this person would stop at nothing until she was dead. Her growing frustration was directed at him, but it was meant for the killer. Or at least, he hoped it was.

"My southern accent and drawl are part of who I am. It's not going away. Think of it as your security blanket."

She gazed at him like he was crazy. "Oh, please, just shut up. I'm terrified this person is going to get to me. You can talk Japanese, for all I care, as long as you stay between me and whoever this jerk is."

Gazing at her, he noted she was working up to a full-blown tantrum that was nothing but fear. Somehow he had to calm her. All he wanted was to take her into his arms and pull her tightly against his chest. But that was *not* a good idea.

"Take a deep breath and let it out slowly," he told her. "You need to calm down."

"Fuck calming down. I want at him. I want to kick him in the balls. I want to pull his hair out, and most of all, I want to see him in jail for doing this to me. For scaring me."

It was all Tucker could do not to laugh. The woman was a fighter. But then, being in Hollywood, she almost had to be. You did not want to be on the other side of this woman's anger.

A smile must have crossed his face because, suddenly, she turned on him.

"This is not funny. Truly, if I could, I would take a pair of tweezers and pull out his pubic hairs one by one. By the time I was finished with him, he'd be begging me to leave him alone."

Tucker couldn't hold back his grin. "Miss Woods, if we catch him, I'll give you that opportunity."

If that's what she wanted, why not? The man had disrupted her life and made her feel frightened.

She jerked. "Really? You would? By the time I was done with him, he'd be begging to be taken to jail."

The detective cleared his throat. "Excuse me. I'm here and I'm listening."

Slowly she grinned at Tucker. "For a southern boy, you might be all right after all. But I'm going to hold you to that promise. I get first dibs at him."

"I'm not a southern boy. I'm a southern man. A Texan. And people don't normally mess with me."

She reached out and squeezed his biceps and his heart leaped into his throat.

"I can see why."

Leaning back, he hoped that her meltdown was now over. But he also realized there would be more. The more intent this person became on pursuing her, the more she would freak out. And he couldn't blame her.

Someone wanted her dead and the thought was terrifying.

"Is there anything else I need to file my report," the detective asked, his gaze irritated.

She was right, the police acted like this was just another crazed fan who was all bluff. But Tucker didn't think so. If this stalker wasn't serious, the letters would have stopped by now.

"No," Tucker told him. "Miss Woods is in for the night and won't be going out anywhere. My men—"

"Oh no, that's not true," she said. "I have the dinner at the Plaza tonight."

"Cancel it," Tucker told her, swinging around to face her. "You're safer here at home."

Her eyes narrowed on him. "It's my job. I'm a starlet. The studio is holding a big dinner tonight with the cast of *Secrets of a Summer Place*. I'm playing Jennifer, the main character. I've got to be there."

The detective glanced between the two of them. "If that's all, I'll take this envelope to be analyzed and see if we can get any prints. But I'm warning you, if I learn this is someone on your staff, I'll prosecute them to the fullest extent of the law."

Oh no, not the thing to say to an already suspicious Kendra. A sweet smile spread across her face, but Tucker knew her well enough to recognize that was not a true smile. That was an *I'm going to kick your ass* smile.

She walked over to the detective, her sapphire eyes blazing with fire. "If this turns out to be one of my employees, I'll host the next Policeman's Ball and even sing at it. That's how certain I am of it not being one of my staff members."

The man licked his lips nervously and Tucker could see he was anxious about how to respond. The man must recognize a thoroughly pissed-off woman.

"Thank you, Miss Woods," he said. He nodded at Tucker and hurried out the door.

As much as Tucker hated to admit it, Kendra had been right about the police. She'd be dead before they took this case seriously.

"As your security person, I'm advising against going tonight," he said to her. The woman was as stubborn as they came, and he could already see from the expression on her beautiful face, that this was a battle he'd never win.

"The car will pick me up at six. Be ready," she said, not even willing to consider staying at home.

"Will there be paparazzi?"

"Yes, tons of them. Lights flashing, cameras shoved in your face, and microphones. Every little thing you say can and will be picked up, so watch your language."

"Cancel the car. We're driving you there," he said.

With a sigh, he knew his men were going to have a long night. "My men will be dressed in tuxes with walkie-talkies. I'll be by your side all night. Where you go, I go."

"Even the ladies' room?"

"Even the ladies' room," he told her.

Shaking her head, she gave a little laugh.

"Why Tucker, I think you're a pervert," she said. "Do you enjoy women's panties as well?"

Staring at her, he couldn't resist the urge to shock her.

"Depends on the woman wearing them. So yes, I love to see a beautiful woman in lingerie."

"Definitely a pervert," she said.

He'd been called worse.

"No, I'm protecting you. Unlike the men's room, the ladies has stalls where perverts can hide. I'll be standing just inside the door in case you need me."

Shaking her head, she started up the stairs. "I want my life back. My privacy. My feeling of security."

How could he respond when he understood completely?

"And you'll have it all back just as soon as we catch this man."

She disappeared up the stairs and he spoke into his radio. "Team meeting in five, except for Colt. Keep an eye on the cameras."

His men trickled into the house and he gazed at them. They were a hardworking group of men he cared for like family. Men he would trust his life with and he paid them well for the job they did for him.

"Tonight, Miss Woods is attending a dinner in the Plaza. Ben, you will drive her there. I'll be in the car with you. Dave will stay behind with Colt. Judd, you will follow behind us."

The men all nodded.

"The attire is tuxes. Be ready at six."

"Yes, sir," they said and returned to their posts.

All his life, he'd depended on what he called his Spidey senses and they were ringing alarm bells. The letter arrived today. Would the creep be so bold as to try something tonight? Could he know about this dinner she was attending?

As much as he longed to turn the protection of Kendra over to Judd, he couldn't. No matter what was occurring between them, he had to be at her side.

Tucker glanced at his phone. He needed to locate the Plaza restaurant. Make certain of the route they took and their exit strategy. Hopefully he was wrong, but it was always better to be prepared than ambushed.

CHAPTER 6

*S*ometimes Tucker hated his job, and tonight was one of those nights. When the limo arrived at the restaurant, his men stepped out of the car and gazed around at the crowd before they turned to help Kendra alight. They moved in around her and circled her the best they could, trying to keep people from reaching her.

This was a dangerous situation and yet Kendra had insisted they attend.

Of course, the paparazzi lined the street and he almost groaned as she waved and walked up the sidewalk toward the restaurant. The dress clung to her and he had the most incredible urge to lean in and smell her. His heart pounded in his chest, and he had to remind himself that he was her bodyguard.

His eyes swept through the gathering, looking for anything that appeared to be the barrel of a rifle or the short muzzle of a revolver. There was no way they could keep her safe in this throng of people, but they were doing their best.

"Let's move," he said into the mic on his shoulder.

Some of his men were in front and some behind as they parted the people to enter the restaurant.

Kendra saw someone in the crowd and leaned over and took her hands and hugged the woman. They needed to get her inside.

"Don't stop," he said as he leaned down close to her ear. "It's too dangerous."

"You can't make me," she said, being defiant as usual. "That's a fan who is always at my premieres."

"Not worth taking a chance," he told her.

"To me it is. I want to be involved with my fans," she told him as she smiled.

"Your choice," he told her. "I'm just trying to do my job. Get you in the building safely."

His fingers touched the center of her back and a heat wave spread from his fingertips to his groin. Why was it whenever he touched her, this warmth filled him?

With a smile on her face, she glanced behind her.

"Let's go," he said. "Keep walking toward the door. Get inside."

She waved to the people and when she reached the top of the stairs, she turned and blew them a kiss.

The woman didn't understand the risks she was taking.

He pushed her inside the door. Knowing that right there was the shot and doing his best to keep her safe.

"Don't rush me, when I'm making an entrance," she said softly, the smile still on her lips, though her tone was sharp.

"Just trying to keep you safe, princess," he said, regretting saying *princess* as soon as the word was out of his mouth.

She turned and grinned at him. "Princess. I kind of like it."

"You would."

Once again, he'd given her an opening and she'd jumped on it like a bass going after a spinner.

With a growl, he shook his head. When his eyes adjusted to the inside of the restaurant, he swept the room. Hollywood elite filled the fancy restaurant. Even some of his former clients were in attendance.

Laying her hand on his chest, she leaned in close. "Sorry, cowboy, but this is where I leave you."

"No, ma'am," he said. "I'm going with you. Like I said earlier, where you go, I go."

Her brows drew together in a frown. "You're a real pain in the ass."

"Yes, ma'am, I am. That's why I'm at your side. That's why you hired me to protect you."

The young man behind the counter smiled at her and Tucker had to resist the urge to keep from pulling his head off.

"Welcome, Miss Woods. Your party is in the Clarendon room," the maître d' said, pointing down the hall. "Have a great evening."

When they reached the room, he looked through the open door before he let her go in. The crowd was much smaller. Relief filled him. Here, he could watch her.

"I'll be standing against the wall, observing, keeping you safe."

"Hardly necessary since these are my coworkers and the heads of the studio," she said.

Everyone was a suspect. Even her agent, Anthony. Everyone.

"They're people and people can be dangerous," he said. "Until we know who this stalker is, I'll be close by. Enjoy the party."

Shaking her head, she glared at him. "Stand back, cowboy, and let me do my job."

"Yes, ma'am," he said. "I aim to please."

She chuckled.

"You should be wearing spurs."

"Then I could not sneak up and surprise people. Everyone would know where I walked."

"True, but just the thought is hot."

Hot? As in sexually hot?

Speechless, he stared at her, wishing they were alone. Wishing she wasn't his client.

"All right. I'm going through the door, but the studio is going to ask me questions," she said.

"Tell them very little," he responded. "We don't know where this guy is and if he's among the studio execs, then that would alert them."

She turned and gave him a weird look. "You've been doing this way too long. The studio executives are not my stalker."

"You never know," he told her knowing his guards were already outside, circling the building, looking for anything suspicious.

When they entered the room, he stepped off to the side and watched as a large man wearing a five-thousand-dollar tux moved to her side.

"Kendra, so great to see you. I'm so excited about this film," he said as he kissed her cheeks.

Like a soldier, Tucker stood on the back wall, his microphone clipped to his shoulder, his men checking in regularly. He watched as she kissed the cheeks of the Hollywood elite.

What was he doing here? Sure, he had safeguarded women before, but for some reason, this didn't feel right. Or maybe it felt like he should be by her side. But that was crazy.

Leaning down, he spoke into his microphone. "We're in."

At least twenty actors and ten studio executives were in the room. Could this stalker have something to do with the movie?

He watched as Kendra owned the room, laughing and talking and being congratulated by the people for her upcoming role.

Soon they sat to eat. Tucker stood like a statue, his eyes on the occupants. One man seemed a little more friendly than the others and that concerned him. One woman seemed to be less friendly and another seemed overly eager to be near her.

Speaking into his microphone, he told his men. "Remind me to get the names of everyone who attended this party and a photo of them. They're going up on the board."

In the cabana house, he'd set up his command center and they had a list of suspects there. He had some new people to add.

She called over a waiter, and he watched her talking animatedly with him. Then she gave him her credit card. What was that about?

He would need to ask her what she said to the waiter. Even staff at a restaurant were suspects. Until they figured out who was after her, everyone she came into contact with was shady.

After the dinner, the head of the studio rose and went to a podium. For the next five minutes, he talked about how excited they were to make this picture. How the compelling story of two young people falling in love had touched the hearts of millions and now it would be made into a major motion picture.

Next, the director, a famous movie star, spoke about how this story had affected him and made him want to make this into a film.

Finally, when it was almost ten o'clock, the party began to break up.

Kendra said her good-byes to the studio executives and made her way to the door. When she reached him, he stepped in front of her.

"On the move," he said into his walkie.

"God, my feet are killing me," she said softly. "I didn't think the night would ever end."

As they stepped outside, a prickle of alarm scurried up his spine. Something wasn't right. Where was the car?

Tucker stopped in front of her as he tried to slow their progress.

"Where's the damn car?" he said into his microphone.

"Trying to get there, boss," Ben said.

"Let's go back inside," he said, not liking the fact that they were standing in the open, waiting. This wasn't good.

A big black SUV slowly came down the street. The window

rolled down and Tucker noticed the man wore a ski mask as he pulled out a rifle.

"What the hell?"

The man leaned out the window pointing the barrel of the gun toward Tucker and Kendra.

"Mayday, mayday, mayday," he screamed into the microphone as he whirled around and grabbed Kendra, shoving her to the ground.

"Tucker," she screamed.

Rounds of gunshots exploded around them as he covered her body with his. Their limo pulled up trying to block the shooter. Bullets ricocheted off the car door where Kendra should have been standing.

People panicked, screaming and running in all directions. For a moment, he feared them being trampled.

Kendra began to wail, screaming and crying. "No, no, no."

Fearful the shooter would locate them on the ground, Tucker covered her mouth with his. A kiss he'd never intended to give became a desperate attempt to quiet her. Slowly it changed into a passionate searing endeavor to continue living.

A kiss that promised life had him pushing out the sounds of the screams as the SUV sped away.

Abruptly he ended the kiss. Lying on top of her, he wondered if he had hurt her when he shoved her to the ground.

She stared up at him, tears had streaked her makeup, her large sapphire eyes were bright with tears and fear and something that even looked a little like desire.

"Are you all right?"

"Damn, cowboy, you know how to kiss. But your timing really sucks."

He ignored her attempt at humor. This can't happen. Over and over again, he'd warned his men about getting involved with a client. He can't be the one to break the rules, but that was a hell of a smooch. Even now, he could feel his dick pushing into her dress.

"I had to keep you from screaming," he said. "I didn't want them to locate us on the ground."

Her lips were trembling as she tried not to cry.

"Please take me home."

Knowing the police would want to speak to her, he shook his head.

"I wish I could, but now we wait for the police."

"What if he comes back?"

That was Tucker's concern as well.

"Let's get you in the limo. The police are on their way. We'll speak to them briefly and then we'll leave. I'll be by your side and the doors will be locked."

A big flash blinded him.

"Hey, stop," he said, jumping up and shielding her with his body, unable to see with the flashbulbs going off.

"Oh no, the paparazzi," she said.

Tears rolled down her face and he understood this had really shaken her. His strong princess was a wilted flower, at the moment.

Like vultures, the cameras flashed and he gathered her against him, his arms around her. These savages would tear her apart with their hands if it would give them a great photo. All his command did was draw attention to them. Now he had to get her out of here and into the car.

"Lean in close to me. I'm going to pick you up and put you in the limo," he said.

Sobbing quietly, she hid her face against his shirt. His heart wrenched as he carried her to the car, his eyes searching for another attack in the crowd.

"Please make this stop. He's going to kill me."

"I'm trying, sweetheart, I'm trying. And I would never let him hurt you. Never."

This son of a bitch had just crossed into dangerous territory and Tucker was going to do everything he could to bring her through this alive. Maybe it was time to consider moving her somewhere he knew she'd be safe.

Somewhere she could hide without anyone knowing where she was.

Maybe it was time to take her home to the Burnett Ranch.

CHAPTER 7

*K*endra clung to Tucker all the way back to her mansion. Tonight had been so scary. Hearing the gunshots and knowing they were for her. The feel of Tucker covering her with his own body had felt good, but also terrifying.

Yes, that was his job to keep her safe, but the man had risked his own life to keep her from dying. And damn, that was so important that she didn't know what to think.

The feel of his lips against her as she melded into his body, the rake of his tongue as he silenced her. Never had a kiss been so explosive, so full of danger, so intriguing.

When the limo pulled up to the house, they drove as close to the door as they could get and then he got out and shielded her body with his as they hurried inside.

A group of men had arrived before them to go through the house and make certain it was safe. Damn, she couldn't believe her life had become this ever-constant threat in need of protection.

Someone was seriously out to kill her.

When they walked through the front door, she wanted to collapse.

"We need to talk," Tucker said.

Right now, she felt the need to wash the fear from her, to calm her rapidly beating heart, and find some normalcy once again.

She held up her hand. "Not yet. Please, I need to go take a hot shower and relax. At the restaurant, I ordered all of you food. It's in the limo. A little cold now, but still really excellent food. You guys eat and afterward, we'll talk."

The men smiled when she mentioned food. She knew they hadn't had a chance to eat all night. And they might need their strength to defend her again, so she wanted to make certain they were fully charged.

"Thank you," Tucker said. "That sounds like a good plan. By that time, Anthony should be here and we can all sit down and talk about what should happen next."

What should happen next was that they should find and arrest this asshole.

She nodded and went up the stairs needing time to herself. Needing to regroup and not let this fanatic win. Glancing around, she wondered if her life would ever return to normal.

Downstairs, she heard the excited voices of Tucker's men, then the footsteps of someone following her. Turning, she saw one of his guys.

"Ma'am, I'm going to wait right outside your door," the young man said. "Tucker asked me to stand guard. You take as long as you need."

Tears welled in her eyes at the thoughtfulness. As she climbed the stairs, she'd worried about someone getting in and reaching her before they heard her screams.

Tucker was so afraid for her that he was posting men outside her bedroom door. Suddenly it felt like her freedom was about to become even more restricted.

"Thank you," she said, walking into her room and collapsing against the closed door.

Who wanted her dead? And why? Knowing she would soon hear from her sister when she saw the news reports, she texted her not wanting to wake her.

I'm all right. Frightened, but fine. And no, I'm not coming to Mississippi.

She went inside the bathroom and stripped out of the beautiful gown she'd worn tonight. It had grass stains on the skirt and she wondered if they would come out. She liked to donate her gowns after she wore them to a shop that catered to young teenage girls looking for a prom dress who didn't have the money to buy one.

It was just a small way she gave back to the community. Long ago, she'd been that young teenage girl who couldn't afford a dress.

Stepping into the shower, she realized she and Anthony would have to talk about how much to tell the studio. They would not like hearing that their main star in this film had people trying to kill her. Their insurance would object and want to replace her.

And she wanted this part more than anything. She'd read the script. It had Oscar written all over it.

Letting the hot water cascade down over her body, she sighed and tried to ease the tension that consumed her. Tonight she could have died. But Tucker saved her. At the sound of gunshots, she'd felt herself being thrown to the ground. Tomorrow there would be bruises, but she was still breathing. Her heart was still beating.

After standing under the spray for thirty minutes, she crawled out and dried off. Right now, she wanted comfortable clothes. She needed the cuddly feeling of her big fluffy robe and her silliest pajamas. Tonight, she chose the pair that had big red pouty lips all over them.

Combing out her wet hair, she smiled at the thought that the security team was about to see Hollywood's biggest actress without makeup, wearing a robe, and her hair still a wet mess.

She didn't care. Nothing mattered right now but her comfort.

After she'd put on some night moisturizer, she came back down the stairs.

In the den, she heard Anthony's voice.

"She's not going to like that idea. Especially with this new film coming up soon."

"It's the safest place for her," Tucker replied.

"All right. I'll back you up, but I'm just warning you," Anthony said.

"If you'd seen the terror on her face tonight, you'd agree that this is the best thing for her."

With a sigh, Kendra walked into the room, figuring they were about to present an idea she would not like. Right now, she didn't have the energy to combat them. Tonight the fight had fled from her at the sound of those gunshots. One bullet had landed on the ground near her.

That bullet had been intended to kill her.

"I'm pretty sure the paparazzi got a candid shot of me lying on the ground beneath Tucker screaming until he kissed me," she said, walking into the room.

Every man in the room glanced up and stared at her and then at Tucker.

"I had to do something to quiet you down, so they couldn't target us on the ground," Tucker said.

His face looked pained like he hadn't enjoyed the kiss at all.

That kiss had not meant anything to him. Just part of his job description. Damn, she'd really liked the feel of his lips on hers.

Anthony's head swung around. "What? You didn't tell me that part, Tucker."

"I had her down on the ground, covered, but I didn't want the gunman to know our location and possibly shoot me in the back, which would have then hit her. So I did what I had to do," he said.

Anthony glanced between the two of them. "The way you two go at each other all the time, I'm not worried. There's mutual dislike between you."

That wasn't true. She found Tucker to be a very attractive man. If she were capable of dating, she would ask him out. But that wasn't possible. Not with her lifestyle. Not with his lifestyle.

"So what do we do now? The police have a description of the car. You can't see the gunman's face because he wore a ski mask. What happens next?"

The two men glanced at one another. Why did she get the feeling this was going to be something she didn't want? They had that guilty-as-sin look on their faces.

"It's time for you to get out of Hollywood for a while," Tucker said.

"Okay, but where would I go? I'm not going to my sister's and endanger them. And even if I leave, who's to say he won't follow me."

Walking to the couch, she sank onto the cushions, pulled her legs up under her and tucked them beneath the terry cloth robe. Inside, her nerves were tenuous. Even now, she felt like she was shaking.

Anthony brought her a hot cup of tea. "Here, I made this for you."

"Thank you," she said, wrapping her hands around the cup. It was after midnight and she felt her body beginning to sag from the stress of this day. But there was no way she could sleep.

"My family owns a dude ranch in Texas," Tucker said. "I have my own house. Nothing as fancy as this, but a nice three-bedroom house with two baths. I'm back far enough on the property that no one would have to know you were there. In fact, I would encourage you not to leave the house."

Great, another jail cell. Only this time in some wild west hick town. Why was she in jail and not her tormentor?

"And what would I do all day besides stare at the four walls?"

49

"You could memorize the lines in the movie script," Anthony said.

She sighed. She could do that, but still being stuck in a small house out in nowheresville Texas did not sound appealing.

"No," she said. "I'm not going anywhere. I'm going to stay right here."

Tucker frowned. "While we were gone, we have surveillance on the camera of a man coming onto your property. He took note of all the cameras and tested the windows. He cut the wires to the alarm system and found the phone lines. We believe they're preparing to break in. I've put up extra guards to circle the grounds tonight, but you would be safer at my ranch."

She put her hand to her head and rubbed her forehead. How could she ever feel safe in this house again? Who were these people, and why in the world were they after her?

"Do you have any idea of who this could be?" Tucker asked.

"Show me the pictures," she said, wanting to kick someone's ass.

Tucker had printed them off and he handed them to her.

She glanced through them. None of them looked familiar. No one. In fact, they just looked like a group of thugs, checking things out to rob her later. Was it money they wanted?

"I don't recognize any of them," she said, gliding her hand through her wet hair.

They knew her security system. They knew her home and they wanted to kill her.

"So if we went to this farm in Texas, when would we leave?"

"Right now," Tucker told her. "My private plane is on standby. And it's a ranch, not a farm. Big difference for us cowboys."

Who the hell cared? Ranch, farm, all she knew was that she was leaving everything she loved behind and going to some Podunk place where buffalo probably still roamed the range.

"We need to call the studio," she told Anthony. "They're going to want an explanation of what happened tonight in front of the restaurant."

Anthony nodded. "I'll take care of that. I'll even tell them you have disappeared for a few weeks in order to memorize your lines."

Total bullshit, of course, but whatever worked.

"What about your men? Will they go with us or stay here?"

"No, they're staying here. I'm hoping whoever this person or group is will be tempted to try to walk in while we're gone. You'll be safe and my men will be here trying to catch your tormenter."

She wouldn't be where he could get to her. While she trusted Tucker and knew he would do everything in his power to keep her safe, she also realized she was vulnerable here.

"Who would be protecting me at your ranch," she said.

"My family. No one gets through our gates without going through the guardhouse. There are twelve men in my family that help run our organization. We all have guns. We all know what to do in case of an emergency. But the biggest thing is that no one will know where you are. There will be no comments made about your location."

It sounded ideal, and yet, she hated to go off and leave her home. She loved living in Hollywood.

"All right," she said. "I'll go, but please, for the love of God, I'm not going to sit in the house for the next month. I can't do that. I'll go crazy."

Tucker smiled. "How soon can you get packed? We're leaving tonight."

Glancing at him, she remembered the feel of his lips on hers. His kiss had been nice, real nice, until the gunshots started exploding around them.

"Give me thirty minutes," she said, thinking of all she needed and she didn't have the strength to put on makeup.

"Wear something that no one would recognize you in. I want

a big hat on your head. And we will be switching cars at several locations before we get to the airport. These bastards are not going to follow us."

Fear suddenly filled her. Would they shoot at her again once she left the house?

CHAPTER 8

*A*fter Kendra went up the stairs, Tucker dialed his brother. It was in the middle of the night, but he didn't care.

"Someone better be dead," Travis said groaning.

"I'm bringing a security risk to the ranch. They tried to kill her tonight and I've got to get her out of Hollywood. No one can know who she is and where she's located, or they will follow me. Do you understand?"

There was a moment of silence and Tucker knew he must be getting up. "Sorry, I didn't want to disturb Samantha. This security risk is she an actress?"

"Yes, you'll know who when I get there, but I don't want to say her name. They tried to kill her tonight."

"Whoa," Travis said. "What do you need me to do?"

There was so much he wanted to tell him, but the dude ranch had to continue on like normal or it would be suspicious. And if the criminal was smart, he would check out Tucker's background.

"Security needs to be on high alert. No one enters or leaves the ranch without our knowledge. My plane will take us to DFW and then we'll take a helicopter to the ranch. My pilots, of course, are sworn to secrecy. If you'll make certain my house is clean and the fridge has the basics that would be great. Also make certain all the security cameras are working."

Travis started laughing. "Do you remember our wedding? Do you remember Eugenia telling you, you're next? Are you prepared for our grandmother to try her matchmaking skills on this actress?"

Tucker sighed. He'd forgotten all about Eugenia's threats because he wasn't concerned. If only there was a way he could keep her out of the house, but that ghost would most definitely cause trouble.

Maybe he could bribe her by telling her he would date someone else once this was over. Poor Kendra didn't need an experience with a ghost. But he also didn't know how to stop his overeager great-great-great-great grandmother.

Having Kendra living in his house was going to be quite the temptation. One he could not fall into for so many reasons.

The rules applied more to him than anyone else. And yet Kendra was such an enticement.

Already his men were gazing at him with suspicion when she'd told them he kissed her.

"Somehow I've got to stop Eugenia," he told his brother.

Travis laughed. "Good luck with that. Besides alerting the security team, cleaning the house, and getting milk and eggs, what else do you need for me to do?"

"Can you arrange for our meals to come to the house? I don't need her up at the clubhouse with all the other guests. The news of her location would get out and then we'd have a war right there at the dude ranch."

Travis was silent for a minute. Then he gave a little chuckle. "So just you and our matchmaking ghost and this starlet are going to be holed up in your home?"

Oh God, he was right. They would be alone.

"Yes, and I'd appreciate it if you could keep the family away as much as possible. I don't need one of them letting it slip that she's staying at the ranch. Not unless you want a host of bad guys descending on us. Last night, the men were well armed and well equipped."

After watching the security video, he couldn't help but wonder if this wasn't a mob hit. It had the signature elements of a classic drive-by. But why? Once they reached his house, he planned on doing an analysis of everyone she knew. Including Anthony. The man was the closest person to her and he knew where they were going.

But why would her agent want to kill his best client?

"What else do you need?" Travis asked.

"That's all I can think of. Oh, how much ammunition do we have on the ranch?"

"All right now you're starting to scare me," Travis said. "I'll make certain we have a lot and also put a canister of bullets in your home."

"Good. Again, I think as long as no one knows where she is, we'll be safe. That will give me time to research why and who is doing this to her," he said, thinking this was probably one of the most complex cases he'd ever been involved with. "Try to get some rest. It will be noon before we get there. I'll call you when we're close. Have a car waiting for us. Not the jeep. I don't want anyone to see who is getting off the helicopter. Just you and me and my starlet."

"Will do," Travis said. "Remember both Samantha and Emily are pregnant. Please don't endanger them."

"I'll do my best," Tucker said. "But the ranch is the only place I could sneak her in and out of. Tell Tanner what's going on. I didn't want to call him in the middle of the night. Get some rest."

"But you wanted to call me and interrupt my sleep," Travis said.

"Of course," Tucker said.

"Good night, Tucker," Travis said and hung up the phone.

Glancing up, he saw Kendra dressed in jeans, T-shirt, and sneakers standing by the stairs. One of his men had carried down three large suitcases.

"You can take one of those," he said.

"No, I need my stuff," she said. "I'm taking all three."

"You're going to a dude ranch where you will be in hiding."

"One suitcase is work related. Recording equipment. Song writing materials. My computer. One suitcase is my clothes. And one suitcase is dressy clothes in case I have to make an appearance somewhere. Plus, my makeup bag."

Staring at her, he shook his head. "Do you never just relax?"

"No, I work," she said. "It's why I'm successful."

Anthony stood back with his arms crossed, snickering.

"You're not going to win," he told Tucker.

"The plane can only hold so much. And I need to take surveillance stuff and ammunition. The helicopter holds even less."

"I'm not leaving any of this behind," she said, glaring at him.

"Do you want me to leave my guns behind?"

Finally she rolled one suitcase over to Anthony. "Mail this to me at the ranch."

"No," Tucker said. "Nothing can come in with your name on it."

"Then give me a name I can use," she said. "Or make room for my suitcase."

With a growl, he shook his head. "Send it to Desiree Burnett. That's my cousin. I'll tell her I have a package coming with her name on it."

Already, he could just see Desiree's face and when he told her what was in it, she would laugh and think he was ordering dressy women's clothes for himself.

Having Kendra at the ranch was going to be a challenge. A big challenge.

56

He glanced at the team member who had carried Kendra's suitcases down.

"Gather the team."

The man nodded.

Anthony hugged Kendra. "Call me when you get there safely. I'll take care of the studio and give them a brief rundown on what's going on."

"I don't want to lose this part," she told him.

"I'll do my best," he said. "You be careful. I don't want to lose my favorite client."

She reached up and kissed him on the cheek. "Thank you for taking care of me. For always being there for me."

"My pleasure," he told her.

The team had assembled in the front entry hall. Judd, Ben, Dave, and Roger were geared up. Colt was still watching the security cameras. "We're leaving. Judd, I've decided I want you, Ben, and Colt to remain here at the house. Just because we're gone doesn't mean that they aren't going to stop trying. So be prepared. I don't know when we'll return."

The men nodded. "Dave and Roger, you're taking us to the airport. We're going in three cars. At different places along the road, we will stop and switch in underground parking areas where no one can see us. I'll give you the locations right before we leave."

The men nodded. It was a trick they had used before to confuse the paparazzi. They knew the routine.

"The last car will drop us off at the airport. The plane is ready. Get back here as soon as possible."

"Yes, sir," they said and walked out the door to bring the cars around.

Tucker felt certain the house would be under surveillance and fully expected a car to be following them when they left.

If he'd had time, he would have added female decoys, but right now, he just wanted to get to the airport.

The suitcases were loaded in the front seat, so they could be quickly switched. All Tucker had was his duffel bag, but it contained several weapons, ammunition, and a few clothes. He was going home, so he didn't need to pack much.

He wrapped Kendra's hair in a scarf and put a man's safari hat on her. While he was putting her hair up, he kept thinking if only he could bind those full breasts of hers, everyone would think she was a man.

"Are you now going to become my hairdresser as well?"

"Why not," he said. "I'm sure you'd love the look I gave you."

She made a harumph noise as she turned away.

At a distance, she did look like a man, but still all those curves were hard to hide.

The cars were as close to the front door as they could be. His team was behind the wheel as he hurried Kendra out the door and into the back seat.

First part of the operation was done and he sank with relief into the seat as his driver pulled out of the drive. The big gates opened and all three cars drove out.

A few minutes later, lights pulled in behind them. They were being followed. Though he felt tense, he trusted his men and knew they could lose the tail.

"You look tired," he said.

"I'm exhausted," she said. "This is all so unnerving. I'm scared, worried, and tired. I just want to be safe."

Unable to resist, he pulled her against him. "You are safe. I promise you, nothing is going to happen to you. They'd have to kill me first."

A tear trickled down her face.

"Thanks, Tucker," she said. "I'm just ready for this to be over."

At least in Texas, she could relax while he researched everyone she'd come into contact with.

She laid her head on his shoulder and a sense of warmth and protectiveness overcame him. If he felt this way now, how was he going to feel when they were trapped inside his home together?

"First switch is coming up," Ben said over the cell phone.

He pulled down into a parking garage.

The three cars pulled up alongside one another.

"Go," the driver said.

They jumped out of the car and into the next car. The drivers switched the suitcases. In less than a minute, they were pulling out again.

A car fell in behind them.

"We've got a tail," the driver said.

They got on the freeway and soon the tail was stuck in the traffic behind them.

"Last switch coming up," the driver said.

This time, they completed the transfer in thirty seconds. When they pulled out of the garage, no one was behind them.

"Looks like we're in the clear," Roger said on the 3-way call. "Headed toward the airport."

"Do we have to check in?" she asked.

"It's all taken care of," Tucker said. He'd made the necessary calls before they left the house.

A sense of relief filled him when all three cars pulled up to the hangar. No one followed them. They closed the doors before he would allow Kendra to exit the car and then he hurried her inside the plane. Only his pilot was on board.

He shut and bolted the door of the private jet.

"All ready for takeoff, sir," he said.

"Let's go," Tucker told him.

The men raised the door to the hangar and a man came in on a forklift and pulled the jet outside.

Kendra sank back in her chair. "I'm taking a sleeping pill. Wake me up when we get there."

"Good idea," he said. He also wanted to try to get some sleep before they landed. Because once they were in Dallas, he would have to transfer her to the helicopter and hope that no one would recognize her in her hat and sunglasses.

The pilot revved the engine.

Tucker sat back and let out a deep breath. They were going home. Home to the Burnett Ranch. Now all he had to do was guard her and hopefully figure out who was trying to kill Kendra Woods.

CHAPTER 9

*K*endra slept all the way from Los Angeles to Dallas. But when they arrived in Big D, the sun was shining, the runways were filled with planes and even landing was congested.

Tucker had phoned for a car to pick them up on the tarmac and take them to his helicopter. There were big windows that looked out from the passengers' waiting area to the gates and he didn't need lookie-loos recognizing Kendra.

"Time to go," he told her as they opened the door to the jet and the steps went down. "Randy is coming up the steps in front of you. Lean your face down into his back and then I'll be right behind you. We are going to the car."

Shaking her head, she laughed. "My security detail has never been this thorough. I've never felt so protected and so afraid."

"Let's just get in the car and then he'll take us to the helipad."

With a sigh, she leaned against Randy's back, hiding her face. The sun was exceptionally hot, she felt sluggish from the sleeping pill, and yet her heart pounded.

It took less than a minute and then Tucker shoved her into the car.

"Glad that's over," she said, sinking into the cool air-conditioned SUV.

"Is it always this warm?"

The two men in the car laughed.

"Yes, ma'am," the driver said. "Texas, where swimming pool water is more like bath water."

"When can I take my hair down? I'm sweating buckets up under this scarf," she said.

"Not until we're safely in the house."

"And how long will that be?"

"We have a helicopter ride of at least an hour," he said.

Sinking back against the leather seats, she was ready to get to wherever they were going. She was hungry, grumpy, and wanted to collapse. But not in her big fluffy robe. That would be hotter than hades here.

The car pulled up in front of a helicopter.

"Where's the luggage?" she asked.

"Your stuff is traveling by car," he said. "There wasn't enough room in the helicopter for us, my bag, and all the suitcases."

Turning, she glared at him. "And what am I supposed to do before it arrives?"

He grinned at her. "You could put on some of my pajamas."

Shaking her head at him, she sighed. The thought left images in her mind that she didn't need. Her wearing his pajamas and him shirtless. Of seeing all those hard muscles that she'd felt last night when he'd fallen on top of her.

"It's hot. Please tell me you have air conditioning."

"We have a/c and even in-house plumbing," he said sarcastically. "And last year we added one of those bidets."

"Has anyone ever told you, you are a smartass?"

"No one near as refined as you," he said.

If he knew the truth about her, he would know she didn't come from a cultured family. Most of her kin reminded her of hillbillies only without the moonshine.

Staring at him, she wondered how long she would have to live with him in the boonies of Texas. If she didn't like how this went, she would call a car and head to the airport. She didn't need his sarcasm.

"Look, I'm tired. I'm stressed and I'd really like a massage."

"Understand, but unless you want me to massage you, you're not getting one."

She'd kill the bastard who did this to her if she ever found him. What had she done to deserve this?

"We're here. Same procedure. Randy will get in front of you and I'll be behind until we get inside the helicopter, then the pilot will arrange us how he wants. Don't argue with him. Your life is in his hands."

Great. She glanced at the helicopter and realized it was small. Like small enough to only carry three people and the pilot.

The car door opened on her side and she stepped into the blazing sunshine of the Lonestar State. The heat seared her and she wanted to get on the next plane back to California. At least here, the humidity was not as bad as in Mississippi, though the Texas heat was draining.

Tucker pushed up against her from the back and they ran to the copter sitting on the tarmac waiting for them. Suddenly the pilot was pulling her up inside and Tucker climbed in behind her.

The pilot placed her the way he wanted her to sit and she sank back ready for this journey to end.

They shut the door and the pilot took his seat and Tucker moved up to the seat beside him.

"Ma'am, make yourself comfortable," the pilot said. "And if I tell you to move to the center, do it."

"All right," she said, snapping the seat belt around her waist.

The big engine started and the blades began to whirl. Then they lifted off and her heart rose into her throat.

The bird immediately turned and headed west.

"We'll be landing in one hour," the pilot said.

Glancing down at the city below her, she realized that the Dallas Fort Worth area was a large metropolitan city. Not as big as L.A., but still huge. It took them thirty minutes to get out of the city and the pilot was constantly talking to the control center telling them their location. Asking about traffic.

Tucker sat in the front watching everything.

Soon they were flying over countryside and she saw how beautiful it was outside of the city. Below were droves of cattle and even a few cowboys moving the herd.

Curious, she leaned back and gazed out. She'd never been on a ranch before. She'd grown up along the bayou of the Mississippi. Fish, not cattle, was their supper.

She'd sang in the church choir until they kicked her out when she was seventeen for dating a black man. With a sigh, she wondered how Grant was doing.

After she graduated high school, they formed a band and started touring. Because of Grant, she had gotten her start singing. Then a record producer made her first solo album. And with Anthony's help, she started touring.

And now, she was returning to the back woods, but it wasn't Mississippi, but the biggest and wildest state in the country.

Funny how her life had come around. She wondered if Grant could be the one coming after her. After all, their relationship had ended badly.

She hoped it wasn't him because she wanted to remember him for being the good man he'd been to her. She wanted to always think of him as the one who'd gotten her out of Mississippi.

Maybe she should mention him to Tucker.

Suddenly they were descending and she glanced at the pilot and Tucker then back out the window. There was a large mansion on the property, a lot of smaller cabins, and then some homes sitting away from the cabins. There was a large building, a barn, and what looked like a tent.

She'd never expected anything this large.

The helicopter landed and a large SUV pulled up.

"Same procedure," Tucker said to her. "One of us in front and one behind you."

"I doubt that anyone is around here to shoot me," she said.

"No, but I don't want anyone knowing you're here."

Damn, the man always had an answer for everything.

Someone from the car waited to be in front of her and Tucker took up the rear. And they hurried her into the vehicle.

Once inside, she ripped the hat off and shook her hair down.

"You were supposed to leave it up until we were at the house."

"No," she said. "It's too hot."

A chuckle came from up front.

"That's my brother, Tanner, driving the car. And my brother Travis escorted you at the helicopter."

"Nice to meet you," she said, taking her hat and fanning herself.

"Welcome to the Burnett Ranch," Tanner said. "Shame you won't be able to participate in any of the activities."

Right now, she didn't want to join in anything. It was just too hot.

"Yes," she said. "Your brother tells me you have electricity and everything."

The two men in the front seat glanced at one another.

"I even told her about the bidets we added last year."

The men chuckled. They pulled up in front of a nice brick home that would be her jail cell for who knew how long.

"They're better than those outhouses we use to have," Tanner said, laughing.

"Okay, same procedure."

"Oh, good grief. Do you see any people around? All I see are cows."

"Those cattle could be decoys. They could be the paparazzi," he told her. "Same procedure. We don't want any of our guests to recognize you and since you've taken your hair down, someone might realize who you are."

With a sigh, she waited until Tanner was in front of her and then Tucker behind her. Tanner brought in Tucker's bag and a small one of hers.

At least her makeup bag was here and she could brush her teeth.

When they opened the door, the house was refreshingly cool.

"Emily brought you today's lunch. She thought you might be hungry. She also sent a tray of cookies and veggies to snack on."

Whoever Emily was, she would be forever grateful. Yes, she was still on L.A. time, but she was starving. She'd not had anything to eat since last night's dinner.

"Thank you," she said. "I will need bottled water."

"In the frig," Tucker told her. "Whatever you need we can get from the big house."

The brother glanced at her and she realized he didn't know who she was.

"I'm Kendra Woods," she said.

His eyes grew large.

"The singer?" Tanner asked.

She grinned. "Yes, and I'm also an actress."

"Don't tell the wives," Tucker warned. "I don't need them coming down here harassing her or them leaking information to one of the other family members. Some of whom couldn't keep a secret if their life depended on it. And Kendra's life depends on secrecy right now."

Tanner sighed. "Let's hope they catch the creep soon. Now I understand why you've been so protective." Tanner gestured toward her. "I saw on the news this morning what happened last night. Pretty scary."

Kendra whirled to Tucker. "Oh, on the way over here, I thought of someone who might be upset with me. He started the band that I first belonged to. I don't know what's happened to him."

"Who?"

"Grant Jones," she said. "But it's been years since I spoke to him."

"Some people can hold a grudge for a long time."

"Yes, he was very upset with me when I agreed to make a solo album and went my separate way from the band."

Tanner took her bag and put it in the main bedroom. Tucker opened his duffle on the dining room table.

She couldn't help but stare at all the guns in that bag.

"Are you expecting a war?"

"God, I hope not, but I'm prepared," he said. "And after last night, I'm not taking any chances."

"I put her bag in the primary bedroom," Tanner said with a grin.

Kendra frowned. "No, I'm taking one of the guest rooms."

"The guest rooms are located away from the main bedroom. I'd prefer if we both slept in guest rooms. I don't want you too far from me."

"That's fine, but we're not sharing a bedroom," she said and walked down the hall.

"Good-bye, gentlemen," she said as she hurried to choose where she would sleep.

Tanner tromped out the door, grinning at his brother. Typical sibling. Things might have been different if she had brothers.

The first room she came to had a big window.

"Not that one," Tucker said.

"I would have enjoyed staring out that window," she said.

"This bedroom," he said, walking up behind her.

"Well, damn, the window in this one is small and high up."

"That's right and no one will be able to climb in without us hearing them," he said.

Once again, he was right. This was what she was paying him

for and yet she wanted sunlight. She would need to be near the windows or go bat-shit crazy.

"All right," she said.

Suddenly, the smell of lavender filled the room and she wondered where it was coming from.

"I'm going to rest," she said.

"Good idea," he said and hurried out of her room.

The smell dissipated immediately. That was odd. Did he have a candle in here that smelled of that soothing scent?

CHAPTER 10

$\mathcal{T}$ucker watched as Kendra closed the bedroom door and felt relief. He walked into the living room, knowing the ghost followed him.

The smell of lavender was strong as she came into view.

All he needed was for Kendra to realize there was a ghost and go flying out of here screaming.

"Eugenia, I'm begging you. I will date whoever you find for me if you will just stay away while my client is here."

The ghost hovered above him, smiling.

"Client? You mean that beautiful young woman you have staying in the guest room? I was hoping that I could match the two of you. She seems like a very nice woman."

"She's not. She's mean and vile and someone you would never want me to have as a wife. She's a movie star. An actress who's probably slept with half of Hollywood."

He was lying, but he had to keep Eugenia out of this. She could not be interfering in his life right now. Kendra was not the person she should be trying to match him up with.

"I promise you, as soon as she's gone, I'll date whoever you want. Your choice."

"And you'll marry them?"

"I didn't say that," he said. "I said I would date them."

The ghost glanced at him. "I'm not liking this deal. Why would I take it when there is a beautiful woman just down the hall."

"Do you understand about Hollywood? About actresses? The press? If the newspaper finds out she's here, then all hell is going to break loose. It will harm her. So she's hiding here until I can assure her safety."

"All the more reason she needs you," she said.

Before Kendra went into the bedroom, she had given him a name and he was dying to check him out. But instead, he was talking to a dead person.

"No deal," Eugenia said.

How else could he bribe her into leaving Kendra alone?

"If you interfere while she's here, I'm going to call a ghost hunter. And Samantha knows plenty. We will perform an exorcism to get you out of the house and keep you in your grave. Do you understand me?" he said trying to be stern.

He knew exorcism wasn't the right word, but he didn't know the right one.

The old woman cackled. "Nothing is going to stop me from making certain that my family finds love and gives me more grandchildren. Nothing. No ghost hunter or this exorcism, nothing. I'm a grandmother on a mission and that is to get my grandsons married."

When would the woman get enough?

"What about Desiree? Don't you think you should try to find her love?"

The woman shimmered. "Her turn is coming. But, right now, I'm focused on you and you're the one who brought a woman home."

"She's not the right person," he said, thinking how she could be if only their lives weren't so different.

"I'll be the judge of that," she said. "I tell you what. For the next week, I'll just watch the two of you and make my own determination as to whether or not she's right. But first, I need you to tell me you're not attracted to her. And don't lie to me because I can tell."

What did he say? He'd have to be dead not to be attracted to her.

"I'm a man. Of course, I find her attractive, but right now she's vulnerable and I have sworn to my men that I will not get involved with a client. It's against the company rules."

Eugenia burst out laughing. "Rules? Men don't follow the rules when there is a beautiful woman concerned."

The ghost was right, but still he would be held accountable. As he should be.

"No, I fired a man for not following the rules, and my whole team would disown me if I get involved with Kendra. And she doesn't need the pressure right now."

The ghost shimmered and it seemed like she brightened whenever she was pleased.

"And that restraint makes you a good man. Again, I'll give you one week and then I don't give two hoots and a holler about your restraint. You need a wife and there's a beautiful woman staying here at your place."

Maybe he could find her stalker in the next week and have her back in Los Angeles before Eugenia determined that she was the one.

"Please, Eugenia, her life is in danger and that's why she's here. Nothing more. I'm working to find her stalker. I don't need your shenanigans making my job even harder."

The ghost laughed. "You've got one week and then I'll let you know my determination. If she's the right one, the deal is off."

"No putting her in danger," he said as the ghost disappeared. He remembered how she had put Emily in danger with the wild bull. At least Kendra would not be out and about on the ranch.

Just then his phone rang. "Tucker."

"They struck early this morning," Judd said. "We shot two of them. Didn't kill them, but they're wounded. The police have been taking statements from all of us. Sadly, the paparazzi has been hanging out here. They know Kendra is gone. We've even had news reporters standing in front of her home."

"Damn," Tucker said. "I was hoping that we'd get more time before they realized she was gone."

"What about the two injured? Have they talked?"

Glancing down the hall, he didn't want Kendra to learn this news. Not yet. She needed to rest.

"Can't. One's unconscious and the other one is in surgery. I'll send you a tape of the surveillance camera. I made a copy before the police arrived because I knew they'd want one."

"Good job," Tucker said. "Yes, send it to me. Did they get in the house?"

"No, but the cabana is pretty much destroyed."

"Damn," he said, knowing he would have to tell Kendra.

"I'm sure it was on the news," Judd said.

He would need to brief his brothers and make certain that Kendra was not seen. No one must know of her whereabouts. No one.

"Oh yes, Hollywood Undercover did a ten-minute piece on it," Judd said. "Look, we're cleaning up the best we can and we're going to continue staying here, but I don't think they'll attack again since they know she's gone."

"No, but watch the mail. I'm sure our man will be letting us know how unhappy he is that she's left town," Tucker said.

"Will do," Judd said. "Oh, Anthony said he'd be calling you after he speaks to Kendra."

"Tell him to wait. She's resting right now. She's had a rough night. Give her some peace," he said.

"I'll do my best. Bye, boss," Judd said as he disconnected.

Tucker grabbed his laptop and went outside to sit on the deck. The sun was beginning to sink and it was finally starting to cool off. He'd yet to sleep, but he had to do some research. He had to see the security recording and he wanted to see what the news channels were reporting.

There it was. As soon as he pulled up Hollywood Undercover on the internet, he saw their footage of her home and all the police cars lining the block and the drive.

He heard the door open and she came up behind him.

"Dear God, is that my home?"

He had hoped to let her rest, but it didn't appear that was going to happen. Her home being attacked was a personal violation. One that would eat at her.

"Yes, they attacked early this morning," he said, thinking how they had made the right decision to leave when they did.

She leaned over him and he smelled her womanly scent as she watched the report on his computer.

"What happened," she said.

He gave her the brief rundown that Judd had told him. "The pool cabana is gone. It seemed they thought my men were staying in there."

Fortunately, his men had been on guard last night and had moved into the house, sleeping in her guest rooms.

"This just keeps getting worse. Maybe I should just go out and say here I am."

"No," he said. "All they would do is shoot you."

"But I can't continue living this way," she sighed and sank into a chair next to him.

She gazed out at the landscape. It was nothing but woods. A tear trickled down her cheek. "I'm so tired of this."

It was all he could do not to get up and take her in his arms and comfort her. She'd been through a lot. But he was thankful she'd listened to his advice after the shooting and left her home.

"I know," he said. "But you're safe, and while we're here, we're going to find out who is doing this. I'm going to research this Grant, but I need the name of everyone you have come into contact with. As many as you can remember. Just make me a list."

She stretched her long legs out in the recliner and sipped from a bottle of water. She had changed into a pair of shorts.

"Where did you get the clothes?"

"My purse," she said. "I always carry a change of clothing in my travel bag just in case."

A smile spread across his face. "Are you hungry?"

She gave a little snort. "After seeing my house on the news? Not hardly."

He'd been afraid of that. He'd just received the security film and wanted to watch it, but first, he needed to make certain she could handle the violence.

"Judd sent me the security tape. I wasn't going to let you see it. I haven't watched it yet. Do you want to see it? Can you take it?"

She turned and glared at him. "I'm not a weak simpering little woman, cowboy. Of course, I can take it. In fact, I'd like to kick those sons of bitches' ass for attacking my home."

A slow grin spread across his face. He hoped she was as strong as she said she was.

"All right," he said, setting the laptop on a small table between them.

It started with a big bright explosion and the lights in the house going dark.

"Wow," she said.

In the darkened video, you could see flashes of light which were gunfire. He could hear his men calling out to one another. He heard the 911 call from Judd telling the police they were in an active gun battle.

Then the cabana blew up, sending pieces of the building into the pool.

"Damn them," she said. "When I learn who is behind this, they're going to need a really good attorney."

"No, they're going to need an undertaker," he said and she grinned at him.

"Even better," she said.

On the video, police were yelling. "Hold your fire, LAPD."

Some dark figures jump the fence and disappear into the night.

His men came out of the house with their hands in the air. Standard procedure to keep the police from shooting them.

"I'm glad we left," she said. "You were right."

Turning, he stared at her. "I'm right? Miss Woods, this is the first time you've acknowledged that your security team knows what it's doing."

It felt good to hear her say that, and yet, he didn't want her praise as much as he wanted to figure out who attacked her home. For the second time that day, the thought of the mafia came to him. An individual groupie wouldn't have the ability or resources to blow up a building. There was more to this.

"Oh, shut up," she said. "It's hard to know what to do. You don't want to go off and leave and yet if I'd stayed…"

"If you'd stayed, it would have been even worse. One of us would have been with you at all times, but being in a war zone is not good. Here, all you have to worry about is the paparazzi cattle."

She grinned at him. "Mr. Burnett, I'm not afraid of your paparazzi cattle. I'm sure they'd be really good eating."

He grinned at her. If Eugenia was listening, they would soon feel her matchmaking ways. But she'd given him a week. He was on the clock to find their attackers.

"Call Anthony. He's worried about you."

She sighed. "I wonder how the studio is taking this news?"

"Probably not well," he said.

Tucker stood and walked into the house. They were home;

she would be safe out on the deck this time of night when no one was around.

But how was he going to spend a week with his client without touching her? The woman was gorgeous and sexy and it was all he could do to keep from kissing her lush mouth again.

CHAPTER 11

*K*endra felt this insistent urge to take the next plane back to Hollywood and check her home, but that would be foolish. Sitting here so many miles away was hard, knowing that someone had tried to destroy her house.

Someone broke in with the intent to kill.

Tucker was in the house they shared, putzing around doing something while she stared into the darkness, wondering who wanted her dead.

When she called Anthony, he'd been sick with worry. And she was glad that she'd taken their advice and agreed to come to Texas.

She did indeed feel safe here. Though she knew Tucker didn't want her to leave the house, she would soon go running from the house like a mad woman.

He'd given her a pad of paper and a pen and said to list everyone she knew. Everyone.

How in the hell was she supposed to do that? There were so many people who either worked for her or she was friends with. People who had helped her career over the years and people who she met in the business.

At first, it was easy, but now she was down to scraping the barrel of her existence.

Out beside each name, she wrote how she knew them and if she thought they wanted her dead. Right now, only Grant Jones had motive to hate her. She was tempted to pick up the phone and call him. Let him know that police were searching for her stalker.

But she didn't.

Exhausted, she put the pen down. That's the best she could do.

Getting up, she went inside to see Tucker heating up their dinner.

"You need to eat," he said.

"I finished your list," she answered.

The man glanced at her and a sizzle spiraled down her spine. His emerald eyes stared at her in a way that a man had not looked at her in a long time. In a way that had her blood heating and dancing across her womanly folds making them tingle.

They'd shared that tumultuous kiss when the bad guys were shooting at her, but somehow, she'd pushed it out of her mind.

She'd shoved it down as far as she could, because if she thought about the way he'd felt lying on top of her, crushing her, while his lips singed hers, his tongue scrapping against her own, she'd melt.

Melt right down until they were in bed together.

The man was good. Damn good.

There was no place in her life for a man. None. And yet she longed for children, a family, someone to hold her at night and tell her he loved her. Was it wrong, even with her career, to crave what she realized would be a difficult situation?

The business had her traveling half the year. Where did a husband and children fit into her schedule? And yet she longed for normalcy. The fantasy of being a strong career woman who could do it all was bullshit.

But would her needs be fair to a family?

Tucker Burnett was one strong, handsome man who looked like sin in blue jeans and kissed like the devil himself. For the first time in years, he'd made her long for dreams that could never come true.

Dreams for the family she longed for with a man by her side. A normal family, not the one she'd grown up with.

"I'll get started on it right after supper. I may have to ask you questions."

Gazing at him, she wanted to run her hands up his smooth outlined muscle chest in his tight T-shirt. Those muscles were strong and probably smooth as silk. It was going to be hard living in such close proximity if she continued to torture herself this way.

Swallowing hard, she licked her lips and knew she needed to walk out of the kitchen, but this was his house and there was no place to go. It was getting hot in here and it wasn't because of the Texas heat.

Turning from the stove, he carried two plates to the table. "I did the best I could, but I can promise you, it's not Emily's cooking."

"Whose Emily?"

"My brother Tanner's wife. She's the ranch's chef."

"From what I could see in the air, you have quite the operation here."

"Yes," he said. "Come on, let's sit and have a normal meal."

She laughed. "That's not possible."

Just then her phone rang and she laughed. "See, I told you."

When she picked up the phone, it was from an unknown number. Frowning, she answered. "Hello."

A voice she didn't recognize said, "I'm going to find you. You may hide, but sooner or later, you're going to die."

"Who are you?"

The voice laughed.

The call ended and she dropped the phone.

Tucker gazed at her with a concerned expression. "What's wrong?"

Terror raced through her and she closed her eyes wishing this would end. "It was him."

"What did he say?" Tucker said, picking up her phone. He scrolled through her recent numbers.

It didn't take long to tell him what the man said. It had been brief and to the point. "How did he get my number?"

"It's got to be someone you know," Tucker said. "Someone who has your phone number or someone gave it to him."

That was a chilling thought. Someone she trusted had given this creep her phone number.

Suddenly she was sagging against Tucker's chest and he wrapped his arms around her. "I'll keep you safe."

And while she trusted him, things happened. His chest felt strong and she couldn't help but run her hands around his back. It was solid. Firm as a rock.

Never had she had such strong feelings for a man. Was it because he'd already saved her life twice?

His hand rubbed her back, soothing her. "No one knows you're here except Anthony and my men."

"And that's too many," she said.

"My men are trustworthy."

"Anthony is trustworthy."

He'd never given her any reason to doubt him. They had been together for years.

"Come on, let's eat and then you can go over the list of names with me. We'll see who I think would have reason to want you dead."

The smell of lavender filled the air.

"Why do I keep smelling lavender?" she asked gazing up at him.

Tucker tensed, but didn't respond for a long moment.

"My great-great-great-great grandmother used to wear that smell. I don't know why you're smelling it. Maybe she's come to visit."

She gave a little laugh and stepped out of his arms.

"Sure," she said, thinking that would be impossible. The woman must be dead, so she could not visit.

Though she wasn't hungry, they sat at the table to eat, and she picked at the food. It was really good, but her appetite was consumed by worry and that was a meal that wasn't filling.

After dinner, they cleared the table, cleaned the kitchen, and returned to the list.

"You received the first threatening letter when?"

"About three weeks ago," she said. "It was right about the same time I learned I had gotten the lead role in the movie."

A frown crossed his face and she watched as he made note of what she'd said.

"You don't think me getting the lead role in the movie has anything to do with this stalker, do you?"

"Right now, I don't know, but this started about the same time. Could be a coincidence, but it could also have something to do with the movie."

One by one, they went down the list of names and he wrote down the last time she'd spoken to them.

"Who is Nicole Cohen?"

"She's an actress in the movie," she said, wondering about the young woman. She hadn't known her long, but the woman had hugged her and said congratulations. The woman had obviously lived a full life. She was younger than Kendra, but she appeared older, and for a while, Kendra feared she would get the part.

"How long have you known her?"

"When we both tried out for the same part," she said, wondering again why the girl tried out for the lead. She was younger and a much more inexperienced actress. But then again, maybe she believed in her acting abilities that much. Kendra did not. She felt lucky to get this role.

"Any animosity between the two of you?"

"Not that I know of. She congratulated me and said she couldn't wait to work with me," she said. "Besides, she was there that night at the restaurant. All my fellow actors and actresses for that movie were there."

It would be hard for them to drive-by and shoot her if they were there in the flesh. Unless someone hired a hitman. But would a young, new actress have the funds for that? Maybe it was one of the men in the new movie.

"What about the actors in the film?"

"Patrick Kramer has the lead role. I've never worked with him before, but he was very friendly and told me he was excited to be working on this film with me."

Tucker typed the actor's name into the computer and pulled up information on him. "He's been in drug rehab twice, has a DWI, and been in several fights. But it appears he's been clean for the last two years. Hopefully he's turned his life around and is not doing this for publicity."

"If he were doing it for publicity, wouldn't he hire someone to try to kill him?"

Tucker smiled at her and she felt her heart squeeze. The man's smile was electrifying.

"No, but he might do it to get publicity for the film. For that matter, the studio might."

"No," she said, shaking her head. "I don't want to think they would do this to me, just to drum up sales. It would be difficult to continue to work for them."

"Who else is in the film?"

"Tracy Wasserman plays one of the friends," she said.

He typed her name into his program and shook his head. "She's as clean as they come. Doubtful she would cause trouble."

He scanned the list of names.

"Let's continue on. Tell me about your relationship with Anthony."

"He's been my agent since my first number-one hit. If he wanted to fire me, he would have gotten rid of me long ago. He's stuck by my side and helped me climb to the top. He receives ten percent of my income. I don't think he would do this. He's more than my agent; he's my dearest friend. I'd be devastated."

The very thought brought tears to Kendra's eyes, and Tucker reached out and squeezed her hand. His touch sent heat rushing through her. Why was she reacting this way to Tucker's touch?

"I'm not saying he's the one, but I have to look at everyone," he said and squeezed her hand again before he turned her loose.

Licking her lips, she realized she wanted him to touch her. She wanted to feel his hands on her body. What was wrong with her? She had not reacted this way to a man in years.

"What about Grant Jones?" she asked, more and more certain he was the one behind this.

Tucker typed his name into his computer and then he glanced up at her and shook his head. "He died two years ago of a drug overdose."

"What?" she asked, stunned. "We were together in a band right out of high school. He was my first serious boyfriend."

She closed her eyes and thought back to the kid she'd loved. They broke up when she was offered a deal to go out on her own. Even then, she saw the path he was going down and knew it was time for a break. Many musicians got into drugs and she disagreed with the lifestyle. They were a deal breaker for her and so when the opportunity came along, she'd taken it.

It also led to her first hit single. All these years, she had prayed that he had given up drugs and was doing well with the band. She wondered about the others but could not remember their names.

"I really thought he was the one," she said. "We broke up because I received an offer from a record label and he was doing drugs. No one I work with better ever be caught doing drugs or they're fired."

Tucker nodded. "Agree. They are such a waste and destroy people."

Sighing, she stood and walked around the room, remembering Grant's sweet nature, so sad to hear he was dead.

Tucker came up behind her and put his hands on her shoulders. She leaned back into him, her head resting against his chest.

"Anyone else you can think of?"

"No," she said. "We're no closer than we were before."

"You're safe," he said, his voice so close to her ear that she wanted to turn and let him kiss her again. But she couldn't.

"That's all that's important."

CHAPTER 12

*a*fter the meeting with Kendra, Tucker packed everything away and tried to go to bed. Unable to sleep, he got up and took a cold shower, hoping his body would cool down.

She was his client. He could not kiss her, touch her, and most of all, could not have sex with her. Already, his grandmother had been hovering. Her scent had filled the little house and he knew she was watching them.

That should cool him down really fast. The thought of his grandmother spying on them in the house should help him to keep it in his pants.

His attention had to remain on Kendra and yet not too much attention. How could he control his thoughts and the memory of her sprawled beneath him on a public sidewalk as he kissed her screams away?

The memory of her breasts smashed against his chest, the taste of her, the smell of her, and the way his dick had ground into her center, right there in public kept playing in his head.

If the world had not been watching with the threat of death hanging over them, things would have gone much further.

And yet she'd not said a word. In fact, afterward, she'd been terrified and had stared at him like he had two heads.

She did make the comment that he was a good kisser, but then the fear had consumed her and she'd been shaking in his arms.

Tonight, when she received the call from her stalker, his arms had automatically encircled her, comforting her, and letting her know that nothing would happen to her.

Except from him.

Somehow he had to protect her from himself because with her sleeping in his house, his thoughts were on how she would look naked spread beneath him, of how she would taste and feel.

How did he rein in those thoughts and put them under lock and key?

With a groan, he dried off, slipped on a pair of clean jeans, and walked to the refrigerator. He needed a beer. Something to cool him down and help him relax so he could sleep. Something to tame the beast rising inside him.

As he leaned into the refrigerator to grab a bottle, the smell of lavender permeated the room.

"You're wrong," his grandmother said.

A groan escaped from him. Why couldn't she see that he needed some alone time?

"Grandmother, nice to see you," he said, raising the beer in his hand. He twisted off the cap and brought the bottle to his lips. "We had a deal, remember? You weren't going to talk to me for a week."

She frowned at him. "Is that liquor?"

"It's beer," he said when he finished gulping down a big portion of the contents. His limit was one, not two, with a client in the house. As it was, he was breaking yet another rule.

The rule follower was not doing well.

None of his employees were allowed to drink on the job, but

this was different. He was home and no one knew where they were. And right now, he needed this little bit of alcohol.

Something to take the edge off.

She pointed her finger at him. "My grandsons should not drink alcoholic beverages."

"This grandson deserves it tonight," he told her. "Now don't you have someplace to be? Like resting in peace or some other kind of nonsense? How about a graveyard party? I bet you're missing out on dancing with the corpses."

The woman laughed. "You are a cocky one, that's for sure. Don't you want to know what you're wrong about?"

There were so many things he was wrong about, that he wasn't curious to find out which thing she'd found out about him.

"I'm certain you're going to tell me and then I hope you'll be gone," he said. "It's been a long stressful day."

The woman frowned. "What is stressful?"

How did he explain the world to a ghost who didn't have a single thing to worry about?

"That's when you barely get your client out of the house before they were attacked and killed. That's when you try to hide her as she rushes from one airport to another and have to jump on a helicopter. That's when your grandson refuses to date the woman you've chosen for him and you can't persuade him."

The woman shook her head. "I don't have a clue what you're talking about. Airports? Helicopters? This century is really strange. But I do understand about disobedient grandsons."

"You're telling me," Tucker said and went out onto his screened-in porch and sat in a rocking chair.

The ghost followed him outside.

"But I know that you will come around to what I'm about to say," she told him.

"Oh yes, Grandmother, your request is at the top of the list right now. Right below finding out who is trying to kill Kendra."

"Someone is trying to kill her?"

"Yes, that's why she's here," he said. "That's why I don't give two fiddles about you wanting me to date her or anyone else. I have to protect her."

For a moment, the ghost was silent.

"I'm not worried. You're very good at what you do. But what you're wrong about is that young woman in there. She likes you," she said.

Why did the ghost think this was big news? The problem was that not only did Tucker like her as well, but it was against his business ethics. And right now, he feared one touch and he would go up in flames.

"I'm glad," he said. "After all, I'm keeping her safe."

"No, she's the perfect choice for you as a wife," Eugenia said.

"You promised me a week," he said.

"I was lying," she told him. "Now about her becoming your wife."

"You lied to me? Your grandson? The person you want to trust to find him that special someone?"

He was being sarcastic and he didn't think the ghost realized it. But right now, he didn't care. He had a mission to solve and he had to figure it out and soon.

"Yes, I lied to you. Now let's get serious about Kendra becoming your wife."

He laughed. Somehow he had to keep the ghost from trying to match them.

"No, she's not for me. She's a career woman whose only focus is her singing and acting career. I want someone who wants a family, kids, and wants to make me happy," he said thinking that would be so hard for Kendra.

The woman was very good at what she did. Her voice was beautiful and her acting would one day win her an Oscar. But her life was centered on her career, not on having a family of her own.

The ghost shook her head and put her hands on her hips. Oh no, he could tell she was getting serious.

"Are you telling me that you don't find her beautiful and smart? Or that you don't want her?"

Damn! How did he get out of this? Anything he said would be a lie. Maybe it was better to be truthful and hope she would understand.

He took a swig from the beer bottle. If he could get some peace, he would finish off the bottle and then go to bed.

"Of course, she's beautiful and smart. You have to be both to make it as far as she has in Hollywood. Want her?" He took another drink from his beer bottle for courage. "I'd have to be dead not to want her. But she's a client and she's vulnerable. It would never work. It's against my company policy."

That should satisfy her.

"Company policy? That sounds like something Rose would use to keep people apart."

It was the same, but he would never admit that to Eugenia.

The ghost smiled at him and laughed. "You men have so little faith in us women. If we want something, we'll find a way. If Kendra falls in love with you, she'll make it work."

Having a celebrity for a wife was not something he had ever considered, and frankly, from the people he had protected in the past, divas and selfish bitches were not the right kind of woman for him.

Kendra was demanding, forthright, and had a mouth on her that he often wanted to shut up with a kiss. But he was doing his best to avoid her smart, sassy lips.

"Eugenia, please don't meddle. This is not the right time," he said, worry churning his gut. If his emotions became involved, then his job would be even harder, and he could take risks that might get him killed. Or even worse, get Kendra killed.

"It's the perfect time," she said. "You're both here, together and I'm going to help you."

Oh no, how could he stop her? That's all he needed was a ghost to get in the way.

"No, Eugenia, don't interfere," he said, getting frustrated. "We agreed that I would date anyone you wanted when this was over. We're sticking to that rule."

"Oh no, we're not," she said, and *poof*, she was gone.

A noise had him glancing up. Kendra stood in the doorway in a silk robe that clung to her curves. Oh, to be that piece of silk.

Not what he needed right now. His dick had just gone down, and now staring at her, it was rising once again.

"Who are you talking to?"

He'd drank the beer just a little too quickly and now the effects were making his tongue loose.

"My grandmother. Remember me telling you lavender was her scent?"

Kendra gazed at him. "I'm beginning to think you're drunk."

"Oh no, ma'am. I don't drink around clients. But tonight, I couldn't sleep and so I got up and grabbed a beer."

"Why couldn't you sleep?"

He glanced at her and shook his head. Did the woman not realize the effect she had on him? Had she not felt anything that night they kissed?

"You tell me. I have the most beautiful, sexy woman sleeping beneath my roof. But she's a client. Someone I can't touch, and yet I want to pick her up and carry her to bed, rip that robe off her and explore every inch of that luscious body you have hidden."

A giggle escaped from Kendra. "My, my, Tucker. Yes, you are drunk. Because your client has been nothing but a pain in the ass to deal with all day."

Why did she think that?

"No, ma'am. Why do you say you've been a pain in the ass?"

"Oh, because we had to rush out of my house, dodge the cars

following us, get in a jet and fly out here. A prank call that makes me distressed. It's been one thing after another today."

"That it has," he said. "But you handled it way better than most of my clients."

"You're drunk," she said, laughing.

"No, I'm buzzed. Really buzzed."

"And that's why you're talking to your dead grandmother?"

"No," he said. "She was here. Sit down and let me tell you about her. Because knowing Eugenia, you're going to meet her."

"She's dead."

Kendra slid into a chair next to him.

"Yes, so? She likes to play matchmaker. In order to keep the Burnett family line from being extinguished, she comes back from the dead and matches you up with someone she thinks would fit into the family."

Kendra shook her head. "Wow, you have quite the imagination. You should have been a writer."

Staring at her, he wondered if she knew what was about to happen between them. Because it appeared to him that there was a locomotive on the tracks headed straight for them and he was trying to rescue her.

"No, darling. She's here. And she thinks it's time for me to get married."

"Oh," she said. "Who to?"

"You," he said, laughing. "She likes you."

Kendra's eyes rose and she stared at him.

The liquor was talking and yet he couldn't help himself. He was trying to thwart Eugenia's efforts. Maybe Kendra would tell the ghost no.

Just then Eugenia swirled through the air and came to sit across from Kendra. It was all Tucker could do to keep from laughing at the shocked expression on Kendra's face.

"Hello, Kendra. I'm Eugenia Burnett. Nice to meet you," she said. "Tell my grandson you like him."

For a moment, Tucker thought Kendra would jump up and run through the house screaming. But then she glanced at him and shook her head.

"I thought he was lying. I thought he was drunk. But you're real."

CHAPTER 13

*K*endra had breakfast and coffee out on the patio watching the sun rise before the rays became so hot, the heat drove her back inside.

She had forgotten how much she enjoyed sitting outside until the sweat began to roll off her and she'd gone in, unwilling to be a wilted wet mess.

This morning, she'd read the script once again and set about memorizing the first scene until the studio called.

"Kendra, how are you?" Paul Shell said when she answered her phone. The president of Shadow Works Studio was on the phone with her.

"Paul," she said, her blood racing through her, her heart pounding in her chest. Was he calling her to let her know she'd been fired? Surely Anthony would have been on the phone with her if that was the case.

Why was he calling her now? Was it about the shooting at the restaurant the other night?

Tucker came into the living room and stared at her, his emerald eyes searching hers to make certain she was all right. Warmth spread through her at his concern.

"It's okay," she mouthed. Since last night, every time her phone rang, he was right there and she was glad. Because if she received another prank call, she was handing the phone to him.

He nodded and walked out of the room.

"Anthony told us what's going on. Are you all right?"

"I'm fine," she said. "My security team took me out of town before the attack. I'm so glad they did."

Even though she'd resisted, it was the best decision she'd made since this started. Of course, she wished she could do as she pleased, but for now, this was her life.

"Where are you?" he asked. "I'll send the studio's security to make sure you're safe."

An odd sense of foreboding overcame her, and even though he was her boss, she didn't want to let him know her whereabouts. Tucker had warned her not to tell anyone, including her sister.

"No need," she said. "Anthony hired Burnett Security and I'm safe."

The man didn't pause and she was glad because if he had pressured her, she didn't know how she would have handled his questioning.

"I just wanted to let you know we're worried sick about you. If you need anything at all, please don't hesitate to contact me," he said.

She smiled into the phone. "I've been working on the script. Since I have nothing to do, I thought this would be a good time to start memorizing my lines."

Maybe this was just a call to check on her, but somehow, she wasn't certain.

"Good idea," he said. "I've got Nicole here in my office. She said to tell you hello and that she's worried about you."

"Thank you," she said, warmth filling Kendra. Even her coworker was concerned for her safety.

"If you have to back out of this film, it's all right," Paul said.

"We would switch around the cast and continue on. We completely understand."

Why in the world would he think she wanted to back out? That was such an odd statement. Was he worried about her being on set and maybe endangering the other members of the cast?

"No, Paul, I'm so excited about doing this film. My security team is working hard to catch this person and once we do, I'll be ready to go. I expect this to be over before we start filming."

She wanted to reassure him that this was not going to be a long-term problem.

"As long as you're sure," Paul said. "We don't want to lose you, but I want you to be safe as well."

"I'm fine and I'm getting lots of rest and relaxation."

Not to mention, she had a hot bodyguard who was tantalizing her by going without a shirt. Last night sitting out on the porch, she'd been tempted to reach over and let her fingers trail down his ribbed muscles.

Until his grandmother showed up.

"All right, but like I said, let me know if we can be of any help."

"Of course," she said. "And thanks for calling and checking on me."

"You bet," he said and hung up the phone.

Tucker came back in through the door. This morning, he wore a shirt, but last night, he'd been sitting out on the covered deck without a shirt. Talking to his ghost of a grandmother, which she still could not believe.

And then he told her his grandmother wanted to matchmake them. Oh good grief. This morning, she wondered if she'd dreamed their talk last night. Especially when he told her what he wanted to do to her.

And she'd been tempted to let him.

Part of her wanted to get up and sit in his lap. But then she stopped herself, especially when the ghost appeared.

He came into the living room. "I'm not being nosy, but I want to know who talks to you. Who is in contact with you that might be our stalker."

It was a reasonable request considering that he was working hard to rule out those she trusted.

"That was the head of the studio, Paul Shell. He offered to send a security team from the studio, which I told him no need. He asked where I was and I didn't give him my location. Something warned me not to."

"Good," Tucker said. "We don't want anyone to know."

"There was one thing weird about the conversation. He told me that if I needed to back out, he understood. I'm not backing out of doing this film. This script is a beautiful story and I'm going to play Jennifer."

"Why would he think that?"

"I don't know," she said. "How long do you think I'll be here?" she asked, knowing it wouldn't take long for her to be bored out of her mind.

"I don't know, but I have my entire team researching the list of names you gave me last night. I went over the ones I thought could be problems, but nothing suspicious so far."

With a sigh, she sank back down onto his couch and pulled out the packet of pages. "At least I will have time to go over this script."

Tucker's phone went off and he raised it to his ear. "Tucker."

He frowned as he listened to the man on the other end. She could tell it was a man but had no idea who. At first, she was only casually interested, but his next words sent a tingle of anxiety spiraling through her.

"Read it to me," he said.

Glancing up at him, she saw the concern in his eyes.

"Son of a bitch," he said. "And the police have no idea who this ass is?"

The man said something to him and she could see his frustration.

"No fingerprints?"

The person on the other end replied.

"Of course not," he said. "As long as the police know another one was received, then you've done all you could. Can you tell what magazine they used to cut out the message?"

Another creepy letter had been received. She would never look at her mail in the same way ever again.

"All right, thanks, Judd, for letting me know. Keep me posted on anything you see or hear," he said as he hung up his cell phone.

Shaking her head, she gazed up at him. The T-shirt he wore fit his well-muscled chest to perfection, making her long to run her hands up and over that wall of flesh and then tug his mouth down to hers.

Why did she keep thinking of him this way?

"Another envelope was in today's mail," he said.

"What did the creep say this time?" she asked. Funny how this one didn't bother her. Maybe it was because she was so far from Hollywood. Maybe it was because they seemed to be arriving on a regular basis now.

Tucker licked his lips and shook his head. "They're getting worse. He's becoming desperate because we've outmaneuvered him."

"What did it say," she asked, curious and not curious at the same time because she would dwell on the creep's words and that worried her.

"You won tonight, but when I find you, I'll torture you bitch before I kill you."

Taking a deep breath, she tried to release the fear and frustration. If only she knew the reason why this was happening.

Had she hurt someone unintentionally? She hoped she treated everyone who worked for her well. Last year when her maid's son needed surgery to put tubes in his ears, she'd paid for the procedure because the woman didn't have the money. And that child deserved health care.

Every year, everyone who worked for her received a nice Christmas bonus to help buy their loved ones gifts. Even her accountant, her secretary, her hairdresser and makeup artist were paid well for their time.

So who hated her?

She did her best to keep her political and religious views to herself because people loved to hate actors and actresses for being part of the liberal media. She just wanted to entertain; she didn't care about the rest. But the mainstream media liked to criticize entertainers for the money they made.

Though they made millions telling lies.

With a sigh, she put her face in her hands. The couch cushions sank and Tucker's hands pulled her into his arms. She wrapped her body against his and sank into him.

This was a place she could stay forever. A place she felt safe and secure and he would give his life protecting her. He'd already proven that twice.

"Torture," she said. "This guy is a real sicko."

He didn't say anything but continued to hold her and rub her back.

"Believe me, he's not going to get to you. The only way would be if I was dead and my two brothers would help me. Forget his nonsense because he'll be dead if he attempts to come here."

She leaned back and stared into his emerald eyes. "I believe you. But the thought of someone wanting to torture me is just frightening."

His hand reached out and he pulled her face until she could only look at him. "Not going to happen."

And then his mouth lowered to hers and she wanted to taste him again. She wanted to kiss him. She felt like she'd been waiting forever to feel his lips on hers. His mouth consumed hers. It wasn't just a simple brush of lips against one another, but a demanding *I've got to have you right now* kind of kiss. One she had not experienced in forever.

He pushed her back until she was lying on the couch, her hands came up to caress his face to hold him there, to let him know she was just as involved and wanted this kiss as much as he did.

Lying on top of her, his manhood ground into her and she began to pull at his shirt, needing to touch his flesh. To feel his hard muscles.

Suddenly he pushed back.

He jumped up from the couch and she touched her swollen lips with her fingers.

"We can't," he said growling. "You're my client and I fire my men for getting involved."

Then he turned and hurried from the room.

The smell of lavender filled the area and she heard the old woman chuckle.

"Good job, Kendra. I told him you were the woman for him," the ghost said before she departed. "Keep kissing him and he'll soon come around."

What the hell had she gotten herself into? She was staying with a man who was supposed to be her bodyguard and he had a matchmaking grandmother ghost living in his house.

A ghost who wanted her and Tucker together. But was that even possible?

With a sigh, she sat up. That kiss had knocked her to her knees. She couldn't remember the last time she had enjoyed one so much. She couldn't remember the last time she'd had a man in her bed.

And that was the kind of kiss that normally had two people looking for a bedroom. There were three in this house and she had the urge to try out all of them as long as she was in Tucker's arms.

CHAPTER 14

*T*ucker had avoided being around Kendra since their kiss a couple of days ago. He didn't like going off and leaving her alone, but he needed to talk to Travis or Tanner or both. Anyone but Kendra.

And that damn Eugenia was bugging the hell out of him. This morning, she'd laid out his clothes for him and it didn't include the T-shirt he normally wore around the ranch. It was one of his nice western shirts that he only wore on special occasions. The ghost wanted him to dress up. For what?

As he strode toward the barn, Desiree was walking to him. "Hey, I'm bringing you some food. Emily said to give you the leftovers. There's enough for an army here. Who are you hiding in your house?"

Tucker knew better than to say anything to Desiree. She was a great cousin, but still the fewer people who knew that Hollywood's number one star was sleeping in his guest room, the better.

"Thanks," he said, taking the tray from her. "I'm going to go speak to Tanner and Travis."

She grinned. "You have the look of a man who is running for his life. Has Eugenia shown up yet?"

Stopping he stared at her. "How do you know?"

Desiree laughed. "Remember, she told us at Tanner and Travis's double wedding that you were next. I'm moving out before it's my turn."

He'd forgotten other people had heard the ghost make her declaration that he would be finding love next.

"Oh, I think she would find you wherever you are. She might even drag you home to get what she wants."

Eugenia had spent a lot of time in his home the last few days and he was ready for her to go.

"Do you want me to take that food and put it in your kitchen?"

That was tempting. Kendra had not gotten up yet, so he hoped she would still be in bed. Better not risk it.

"Thanks, but I'll take it," he said, turning and heading back to the house.

"Somethings a foot," she said, grinning at him. "I hope she's everything you want."

And that was the problem. Kendra was everything and more.

Desiree waved good-bye to him and he walked across the lawn to his home. When he reached the steps, Kendra was coming down the stairs.

"Where are you going? You can't leave," he told her.

"I'm going for a run. I haven't exercised. I haven't been out of this house in four days and my brain needs the endorphins. The walls are closing in on me. I've got to get out."

He should have expected this and planned on it. But he'd been busy trying to figure out who was her stalker.

"Your brain is going to get you killed," he said, pushing her back into the house with the tray of food.

"The tension between us is nuts and I'm going crazy," she said, coming right up to him and poking him in the chest.

He grinned at her. "You're welcome. I like to keep my women on edge, and I can see it's working with you."

His women...he hadn't had a real girlfriend in years. Not since the shooter that almost killed him. Sure he often had a beautiful woman on his arm, but normally, it was because he was escorting her and being not only her date, but her protector. And most of those women, he wouldn't give you two cents for. Diva royalty.

She doubled up her fist and hit him in the chest. "Not funny."

Glancing down at her lips, he wanted to kiss her so badly. Seeing her edgy, upset, and admitting the tension between them was getting to her, he wanted to ease that pressure. He wanted to carry her to bed and spend the day exploring all those luscious curves of hers.

Just one night and he could put this behind him. One night of passion.

Taking her by the hand, he pulled her back into the house. "If you go for a run, then one of the guests could see you and we'd soon have the paparazzi cattle taking pictures of you. Can't have that."

"Tucker, I'm serious. I've got to get out of here," she said. "I need some fresh air. I need to move my body."

Most definitely he could help her with that, but then again, that would get him fired from his own company. After what he did to Quinn, he couldn't commit the same sins.

"Ever been horseback riding?"

She frowned at him. "No. Remember my family was poor. We didn't go to summer camps or horseback riding or lessons of any kind. We went fishing for food."

"I've got to speak to Tanner and Travis, but once I get back, how about this evening, we take a picnic and ride horses. I can teach you how to ride."

She smiled. "Really? I've never been, but just the thought of getting out of here is welcome."

He grinned at her. "We have to wait until it's evening because I don't want anyone to see you and the heat in the middle of the day would be too much."

"Agreed," she said. "That's why I was going out running now."

"Am I safe leaving you here alone?"

With a sigh, she groaned. "All right. I'll take care of some business and look forward to us going out later this afternoon."

"Good," he said. "Now, here, put this in the refrigerator. Emily sent us a meal."

"Great," she said. "That woman can cook. I should steal her from you."

"She's married to my brother. She's not going anywhere," he told her and was so tempted to lean down and kiss her upturned face. He had to stop having these kinds of thoughts.

With a wink, she whirled around and he could swear the woman was walking with an extra twist to her behind. Just watching her walk to the kitchen had him groaning. What was he going to do?

Turning, he all but ran out the door, hoping Tanner was in the barn preparing the horses for the morning ride.

When he reached the barn, he stepped inside. "Tanner?"

"Back here," his brother called. Since he'd been married to Emily, his PTSD seemed to affect him less and less. It was now weeks, instead of days between his episodes, and Emily would sing to him and it brought him back right away.

Just looking at his brother, he could see the changes in his mannerisms, the way he seemed more at ease around people and animals, and Tucker couldn't be happier. The man was more relaxed and happy, and in five months, his first child would be born. Tanner and Travis both would soon have children. Babies. And he couldn't even imagine that responsibility.

"What's up?" he asked. "How's your house guest?"

"Driving me crazy," Tucker admitted. "Do you know what it's like when a beautiful woman that you want is staying in your house? And I fired an employee for getting involved with a client. I can't and yet I walk around in a state of hardness all the time."

Tanner hung the saddle on the wall, and then turned and grinned at Tucker. "It's only been four days."

That was the worst part. There was no telling how long she would be staying with him and he didn't know how much longer he could hold out. And she wasn't turning him down.

"I know," he said. "How did you manage around Emily?"

Tanner laughed. "I didn't do very well. Remember we were the ones that were on the video in the kitchen."

Tucker started to laugh. "I'd forgotten about that."

"So are you serious about this girl? I remember Eugenia saying you were next."

"She's an actress. A singer. The most popular person in Hollywood. She doesn't want a cowboy-turned-security owner in her life. She needs a leading man."

Last night as he tried to fall asleep, he'd listed all the reasons they could never be together. The excuses why he could not get involved with her, but this morning when seeing her, all those excuses disappeared.

"Don't discount yourself. You're just as rich as she is. A billionaire with a very successful company. But can you live with that type of attention on you always? Everywhere you went the media would be following."

He sighed. That was the most difficult part if he did have a relationship with Kendra. Could he live with the constant paparazzi taking pictures of them and their family if they had one? But who was he kidding? She didn't want a guy like him.

"I'm just not certain I'm the right person for her," he said. "Don't get me wrong, I will die trying to protect her, and I've never felt so attracted to a woman before. Hell, last night she came outside in a silk robe that reached just above her knees. That silk clung to her flesh like a second skin and it was all I could do not to rip it off her. And then Eugenia showed up."

Tanner started laughing just as Travis walked in. "Family reunion?"

"Just listening to Tucker's woes," Tanner said. "All I know is I'm so glad that I'm married and not going through what you're having to deal with. Don't get me wrong, dealing with a woman's pregnancy is not easy, but I'm not walking around in a constant state of arousal."

"Married life is good," Travis said. "I never planned on getting married again, but damn, I'm grateful that Eugenia brought us together."

Tucker shook his head. "Kendra is the most sought-after singer/actress in Hollywood. Why would she want a cowboy on a ranch?"

As soon as the words were out of his mouth, he turned and glanced around. No one needed to know she was here. Thank goodness the barn was empty except for him and his brothers.

"She's a woman. Samantha had her own television show and yet she loves our life here and is so glad that our child is going to be born and raised at the Burnett Ranch. Give it time, little brother," Travis said. "If it's meant to be, you'll soon know."

He groaned. "I'm a walking hard-on."

Tanner and Travis both laughed.

"She's smart. She's beautiful, and all I can think about is putting my hands on her. Caressing all that soft skin and carrying her to the bedroom. And yet, I'm supposed to be her bodyguard. I fired my best employee because he got involved with a client, and now, I'm resisting."

They both stared at him and grinned.

"I feel your pain," Travis said.

"Nope, not going to say that," Tanner replied. "How's the investigation going?"

That made the situation even more frustrating. "Nothing. I've got nothing. All her friends check out. Her family is a little strange, but she and her sister made something of themselves. I don't know. I have no clues, and yet this ass keeps sending her letters. The latest one said he's going to torture her before he kills her. If I don't end up in jail, it will be a miracle because I want to kill this son of a bitch."

They nodded.

"Our security is on high alert," Travis said. "So far nothing."

"Good," he said. "The head of the studio asked her where she was staying, but she refused to tell him. But why would he want to kill her? She's his star. Honestly, I think it was just because he wanted to send her more protection."

Tanner shook his head. "I don't know. What if the studio is in trouble financially and they have an insurance policy out on their film that if something happened to her, they receive a huge sum of money?"

Tucker stood there and stared at his older brother. "Damn. That's good. I hadn't thought about that. I'll talk to Anthony, her agent. He would know about those kinds of things or at least tell me where to search. You're good, Tanner."

The man grinned at him.

"All right you've given me something to work on. Can I get two horses this evening brought to the house? She needs to get out and I promised her I would take her out riding. At least maybe that will tire us out and I won't be thinking about carrying her down the hall to my room."

"Oh, you'll still be thinking about it," Travis said with a laugh. "You'll be tired, but not too tired."

Tucker shook his head. "Part of me wants this to end right away and the other part wants this to drag out as long as possible."

The two men exchanged a glance and smiled.

"You're in trouble," Travis said.

"You have my sympathy," Tanner replied. "Does Aunt Rose know who is staying here?"

"No, and don't tell her," he said. "That's something I don't need. Desiree is curious, but so far, she's staying away."

Tucker sighed. "I better go. Desiree brought us some food and I ran into her taking it to us. When I went back, Kendra was on the porch about to go for a run. The only way to get her back inside was to promise her we would go riding later."

The two men snickered.

"Do you guys still have the walkie-talkies I gave you for security?"

"Yes," Travis replied.

"I'll find mine," Tanner said.

"Good, just in case I need you. Let's hope this ends peacefully."

"With an engagement," Travis said laughing.

"Or a wedding," Tanner replied.

Shaking his head, Tucker turned and left the barn. Eugenia had matched both of his brothers and they were happy. Could this be his future as well? But not with Hollywood's sweetheart.

That just wasn't possible.

CHAPTER 15

$\mathcal{H}$orseback riding. The man was going to take her horseback riding. She loved horses, but she'd never really been around them. This afternoon, she'd googled how to do it.

She'd watched several YouTube videos and it appeared easy enough.

This afternoon, he'd come back to the house and gotten on the phone immediately. She heard him talking to Anthony and she wondered what about. Later, she was going to ask him.

The heat was beginning to wane when he came into the living room where she was working on the computer.

"Are you ready for your first lesson?"

"Yes, let's go," she said, shutting her computer and rising. She needed to get out of this house. She needed fresh air and some exercise.

He gazed at her and shook his head. "Did you bring any jeans?"

"Yes," she said. "What's wrong with my yoga pants?"

"They're too thin. You go change and I'll find you a cowboy hat," he said.

"Oh, I get to wear a hat?"

"Yes, and boots if you have them," he told her.

"No boots," she said.

"We'll have to rectify that," he said. "But not today. Just wear tennis shoes."

Excited to be getting out of the house, she almost ran to her room. There she changed clothes and put on sunscreen to protect her face.

In fewer than five minutes, she was back out waiting for him. He brought her a cowboy hat that looked like it had seen its better days.

"Who wore this?"

"It's mine," he said. "It's my favorite."

"Oh," she said, thinking the man could afford a new one.

He stood in front of her and stared. "Pull your hair up and put it on top of your head."

"Why?"

"Because it will be cooler and also because maybe then no one will realize it's you. All that long auburn hair is a dead giveaway. I'm trying to keep you hidden here. Oh, and grab a pair of shades."

She returned to the bedroom and pulled her hair up and put on a pair of sunglasses. When she returned, he placed the cowboy hat on her head.

"That's better," he said. "No one would realize it was you until they got close."

"No one will realize it's me with this ugly cowboy hat on my head," she said.

"That one is my best," he said. "I wore it when I was a kid."

He grinned at her and took her hands in his.

"Let's talk about rules," he said. "No talking to strangers. No riding off alone. If I tell you to hide, you do it. If I say get down now, you do it."

"If I say kiss my butt, you do it," she said.

"Honey, don't tempt me," he said, letting his fingers trail down her jaw.

She didn't want him to stop but knew he would. The tension between them sizzled, but he resisted her every step of the way.

"All right, let's go," he said.

Opening the door, he looked outside before he let her step out.

Two beautiful horses were tied to the railing on his front deck.

She walked over and let them sniff her hand. It felt so good to be out of the house.

"How long have you been riding?"

"Since I was five and my brothers were going out riding and I cried because I wanted to go. So my father put me on a horse and I soon learned how to keep up with Tanner and Travis."

Growing up here must have been wonderful surrounded by family and with parents who were normal and cared about each other.

"Your childhood sounds a lot calmer than mine," she said with a shiver as she remembered her family life. Staring at the horse, she asked, "What do I do?"

He led her to the stairs leading up to his house. "Stand right there." He brought the horse up to her left side. "Gather the reins and hold them tight," he told her. "Put your left foot in the stirrup and swing your right leg up and over the back of the horse."

"Why am I on the steps?"

"Because it's easier that way," he told her, holding the horse by the bridle so it wouldn't move.

In one fluid motion, she was up on the back of the horse.

"Hold your reins correctly, between your pinkie and your thumbs. Sit up straight in the saddle. To go forward, you give the reins some slack and squeeze with your legs."

He let go, she squeezed the horse gently and the horse started moving.

"Oh, I'm doing it," she said, turning to gaze at him.

He grinned at her. "When you want to stop, you pull back slowly on the reins."

"It seems too simple," she said.

"It is, but don't worry, I've given you the gentlest horse we have on the ranch."

"Thank you," she said.

He put his left foot in the stirrup and swung his right leg over the horse and settled into the saddle.

"Do you feel comfortable," he asked.

"Yes," she said and reached down and patted the horse on the neck. "I think she likes me."

"All right, let's let them take the lead. Give the reins some slack and squeeze with your legs."

Both of their horses moved across the yard and Kendra swayed in the saddle.

"We're going to ride over to a pond in one of the pastures. There are some trees where we can have our picnic in the shade."

For the next fifteen minutes, they rode the horses across the pastures and she enjoyed seeing the countryside. While the air was hot, it just felt good to be out of the house and enjoying the sunshine.

"I've never been to a ranch before," she said. "I wish you could show me everything."

"That would be impossible, right now," he said. "Come back when the guests are gone and I'll give you a tour."

The thought of returning was a nice idea.

"What was your life like growing up in Mississippi?" he asked.

It was not always a pleasant memory. Her mother worked so hard to put food on the table for them, always hoping that their father would contribute money, but he was unemployed more than he worked. Most employers didn't like it when you came to work drunk.

"We did a lot of fishing, moving, hunting, everything we could to put food on the table."

It seemed like they moved about every six to eight months. The landlord would get tired of them being late on the rent, so he would insist they move when the lease expired or when they couldn't pay. She quickly learned to never get too attached to a place because they would soon be leaving.

And then her mother became ill and nothing else mattered but taking care of her.

"My home life was turbulent," she said. "An alcoholic father and a mother who died of cancer when I was only seventeen."

To this day, she still missed her mother and her sister. Somehow, by the grace of God, she and her sister had turned out all right.

"How did you get into the music field?"

She gave a little laugh and noticed that her horse seemed to know exactly where they were going.

A cow mooed off in the distance and she sighed.

"I grew up singing in the church choir. It was where I discovered how much I loved music. When I was in high school, I sang in the school choir."

Those days had been rough.

"My senior year of high school, my mother died of breast cancer. We barely survived. Then one day, Grant heard me singing in the school choir and asked me to join his band."

It was so hard to believe Grant was dead. He'd been such a great kid until he found drugs. "We weren't dating, but we became good friends. One Sunday, I was singing in the church choir and I asked him to attend. I had a solo that day. The people in church were rude to him, told him he didn't belong there. I've never been so hurt. So I quit the church choir. When I graduated high school, I went on the road with Grant."

She sighed remembering how hard those days had been.

Sleeping in his car or cheap motels, eating junk, and knowing she just had to hang on.

"One night in Nashville, the head of Juke Box Records heard me sing and offered me a record deal. Just me, no one else in the band. Grant was so upset. Sometimes I wonder if I should have held out until we found a record label for both of us, but he was getting more and more into drugs and I believed it was time to leave. This seemed like the perfect opportunity."

Tucker glanced at her. "I'm sorry he died."

"Yeah, me too," she said. "I would have attended his funeral if I'd known. We parted on such bad terms and I always regretted how it ended between us."

The pond came into view and Tucker glanced ahead. "Pull back on your reins and she should stop."

Kendra did what he said and the horse halted. She grinned and felt like she'd accomplished something.

"Hang onto the saddle horn and your reins, swing your leg over your horse, and drop to the ground. I'll be right behind you, to keep you from falling."

She watched as he dismounted and came over to her horse.

"Can't have you falling and breaking a bone. If we had to take you to the ER, someone would recognize you and then the paparazzi would be crawling all over our little hospital."

She grinned. "It would stir up quite the excitement."

"We don't need that kind of commotion around here," he said as he held her horse while she dismounted, close enough to catch her.

When both feet were on the ground, she turned around and grinned. "I did it."

"Yes, you did," he said. "Next week we'll have you rounding up cattle and maybe even calf roping."

"What's calf roping?"

"You chase a calf around in a ring and then you swirl out your rope in a loop, circle the calf's head, and pull it tight against the calf's neck. You jump off your horse and rope tie his legs together."

"Sounds horrible," she said. "Now if you want me to do that to my stalker, I'm game."

He laughed. "It's not bad. As soon as you're finished, you release them and they go running back to the herd."

"I don't like it. It feels like entrapment."

He gave a little laugh. "Come on, let's put down the blanket and start our picnic."

She watched as he ground tethered the horses and then took a blanket out of his saddlebag.

"How did you get into being a security company?"

A frown appeared on his face as he spread the blanket and then plopped down onto it. She sat beside him and pulled the food out of the basket that he had attached to the back of his horse.

"While I was in college, we had an active shooter on campus."

"That's terrifying."

His face darkened and he sighed. "He was going from room to room in the tech building, shooting anyone he found in the hall or the rooms until he reached our classroom. We'd heard the gunshots and locked the door, but two of us decided to stand on either side of the door and grab him if he tried to come in."

His fists clenched and she realized his body had tensed. Unable to stop herself, she reached out and touched his arm, rubbing her hand up and down in a soothing manner.

"Michael, my roommate, and I shared this one class together. He stood on one side of the door and I stood on the other. When the shooter entered the room, we jumped him, but the man was prepared. As I tried to pull his arms back behind him, Michael tried to remove the gun, but he got away and whirled around to shoot me. Michael stepped in front of me."

Tucker's fist clenched and she could see even now he was deeply affected by what happened. "He took the bullet meant for me. Michael died in my arms while another classmate hit the man over the head with a textbook, knocked him out, and ripped the gun from his hands."

"Oh my," she said.

"The man is sitting on death row. Seems he was upset with the college, so he went after the students."

Shaking her head, she didn't know what to say.

"Michael's parents were devastated. Every year, we return to where it happened and we visit his grave. He was such a good kid who didn't deserve to die that way. Taking the bullet meant for me."

He turned and faced her and she could see the pain in his gaze. "After I graduated college, I started my own security company and quickly learned that Hollywood starlets and actors needed security more than anyone. So I moved my headquarters out to Los Angeles and now I commute between here and L.A."

Reaching up, she ran her hand over his cheeks.

"I like catching bad guys and making them pay," he said. "Yet, I could never work in law enforcement. Like you know, my clients have to agree to my rules."

"Yes, they do," she said softly before she leaned down and kissed him.

Her mouth moved over his and suddenly she was being lowered on her back to the blanket. His hands gripped her face as his mouth expressed what she knew he wasn't ready to face.

They had been sniping at each other for days, but beneath all that banter, a fire simmered that sooner or later was going to burst into an inferno.

Oh, how she wanted Tucker. It had been so long since she had a lover, and while living with him, she had seen sides of this man that she really liked.

There was a strength of character about him that she admired. The way he didn't care that she was his client or a star and if he didn't like what she said, he gave it right back to her.

She liked the way he teased her. It was like she was a normal person to him and not a star.

The sound of a helicopter penetrated their passion and he stiffened above her.

Breaking the kiss, he covered her body even more with his. "Don't move. I think I have you hidden."

"Who is it?"

"I don't know, but as soon as he passes by, I'll find out," he said. "It must be a guest."

The sound moved on and he jumped up.

"Come on, time to get back," he said.

"But we haven't eaten," she replied.

"Sorry, we took a huge chance coming out here and we almost got caught. Time to get you back inside where you're safe."

"No, I'm not ready to go," she said.

He was trying to pick up the blanket and she was still on it.

"Kendra, you agreed to the rules," he told her.

"Damn it, Tucker, I just wanted a little time outdoors. If you think I'm going to sit inside that house for the next couple of weeks, you are sadly mistaken."

Jumping up, she walked to her horse and he was there at her side immediately.

Letting her put her hands on him, he helped her up and into the saddle. "I'm sorry. But I worry about your safety. I've never lost a client and I'm not about to start with you."

She watched as he climbed up on his horse and then they were riding back to the house.

It was all she could do not to scream.

CHAPTER 16

*F*or two days now, Kendra had barely spoken to him. While he should feel grateful, he didn't. In fact, he was frustrated as hell. As much as he tried to explain to her that they had taken a huge risk that they could not afford to take again, she just looked at him with those big sapphire eyes, her brows would rise, and then she would turn and walk away.

The woman had turned his own home into a jail. Only he was the prisoner and she was the jailor.

He heard her phone ring and he rushed around the corner to make certain it wasn't their perpetrator.

"Sure you can give her my phone number. Maybe we can work on the scripts via either Zoom or the telephone."

Who the hell was she talking to? Who was she giving out her information to?

She laughed. "Of course. Tell her I'm doing nothing so call me. I'm two hours ahead of you guys, so tell her anytime early morning would be great."

She disconnected the call. Dear God, she had just given them an idea of where she was located. Whoever she was speaking to now realized that she was in the central time zone.

"Who was that?"

"The studio, Paul's secretary called and wanted to know if she had permission to give my phone number to Nicole Cohen."

"You didn't tell her where you were?"

"Of course not," she said. "We're going to have a chat either by phone or by Zoom."

"I'd prefer telephone," he told her. "But you did tell her your time zone. That gives her an idea of where you're at. Now she knows you're in the central time zone."

She bit her lip. "I didn't think about it. But it's Nicole. She's an actress, it's not a big deal."

"Everything is a big deal," he told her. "Don't do a Zoom call. Someone might realize you're staying in Texas and since they know you're using Burnett Security, they will have a good idea where to come searching for you."

All he needed was for the woman to identify something about his house and where they were staying. While this was a good place, he also realized that if the perp did any kind of search on him, he would learn that his family had a big ranch in Texas.

"Well, I like seeing the people I'm talking to. So that may be a problem," she said, raising her voice.

Since the picnic, they had been short with each other even worse than before. Anthony was trying to find out about the studio's insurance and who would arrange for that on the picture. He'd been startled when Tucker called and asked if they were in trouble and if this could be the reason that someone was trying to kill Kendra.

"You also like being alive," he retorted.

"Stop putting flowers on my bed," she said. "We're done."

"Don't worry, it's not me," he said. "It's Eugenia."

She glanced up at the ceiling. "Eugenia, it would be a cold day in California before I would kiss him again."

Tucker crossed his arms across his chest. "No, it wouldn't.

Don't lie to yourself. There is something between us. Even now, I could walk over and pull you in my arms and..."

What was he doing? Just the idea was more of a punishment for him than it was for her.

She frowned at him. "Don't."

He grinned and something inside him urged him on. "All I would have to do was get close to you and breath in your smell, touch your soft skin."

"Tucker," she said. "You're not on my good side right now."

He laughed. "Oh, but I could be. Just give me five minutes and we could be..."

Turning on his heel, he strode away. All he could do was stare at her lips and think of the kisses they'd shared. She was such a temptation, and he needed to get her out of here because Eugenia had started her matchmaking shenanigans.

This morning, Kendra's pajamas were in his bed. And he'd been unable to resist smelling them. The scent of sweet woman was all he could handle before he'd tossed them into her bedroom when she wasn't looking.

The ghost had been quiet and that troubled him. Where was she and what was she doing?

The little things she had done so far only infuriated him. His grandmother needed to go.

Later that evening, Tucker sat in his recliner watching television while Kendra sat with her electronic reader in her lap.

Every so often, she would sneak a glance at him like she wanted to say something, but then she would look back down at her book.

The tension was so thick, you could almost reach out and touch it. And it was more than just the fact that she had not been out of the house. This was sexual tension. The memory of her lips, the way her body felt beneath his. Her smell. The feel of her soft skin. Everything was piling up on him, and sooner or later, there was going to be an explosion.

And then he would think about Quinn. Damn, he was going to have to contact him and apologize. Maybe even offer him his old job back. If the attraction had been this strong, then no wonder his best man caved and gave into what he wanted.

Wouldn't any man?

As much as Tucker resisted, he felt his defenses weakening. A man could only take so much.

Suddenly the lights went out, the television went dark, and fear grabbed him.

"Get down," he yelled and he heard her hit the floor and he did as well.

"What's happening," she asked her voice shaky.

He had to get to her, but first, he needed to call for help.

Picking up the nearby walkie-talkie, he pressed the button.

"Code red," he said. "I repeat, code red. No electricity."

He crawled over to her side and shielded her body with his. "Let's crawl into the kitchen. We'll have more protection there."

A whimper escaped from her.

His gun was still in his holster, but he unsnapped it, so he could draw his Luger pistol quickly. Staying low, they crawled out of the living room into the kitchen. With a counter between them and the door, he could deflect a lot of bullets here.

There were no sounds of anyone breaking in, but that could happen any moment. He placed his hands on Kendra's hips and put her against the wall. The pantry was right there and he thought about having her crawl inside. But he liked her close to him. A wall was behind her and he was in front of her.

Outside he heard ATVs racing to the house. For their sake, he hoped they were prepared. The sound of someone walking around outside had him standing and peering out the window. He saw flashlights.

"Good grief, they're going to be sitting ducks with those lights," he said.

Travis turned the headlights of his truck on the house.

Desiree had her pistol out and she was sneaking around the side of the house.

He watched as Tanner signaled them that it was all clear on the porch, then he busted into the house, with his weapon drawn.

"Tucker," he called.

"Check the house. We're in the kitchen. All I know is that we don't have any power," he said.

Tanner kept his weapon in his hand as he walked through the house checking each room.

"Nothing. All clear," he said and came back to the kitchen.

"What the hell happened?" Tucker said.

"Come on let's check the garage," Tanner said.

"Stay here," Tucker told Kendra.

They entered the garage and Tanner held up his flashlight to the breaker box. "Someone turned off the power."

Glancing around the garage, Tucker stared. "Who?"

Suddenly the smell of lavender blasted him in the face.

"Dear is something wrong?" his grandmother asked.

And he knew. "Eugenia, did you turn off the power?"

"What? Me? All I did was flip that switch," she said. "I watched the electricians in the barn and learned which one turned off the power. I wanted you and Kendra to have some time alone in the dark. I thought it might bring you closer."

His heart was thrashed in his chest and it wasn't because he was filled with desire. He'd been terrified he'd missed some clue and that Kendra's life was in danger.

"Eugenia, I swear to God, I'm calling a ghost hunter in the morning. Kendra isn't safe and when you turned off the lights, I thought the bad guys were here. I thought I was going to have to defend her life."

"Oh, that's so sweet," she said. "You guys have not been getting along and I wanted to bring you closer."

A giggle could be heard behind him and he whirled around to

see Desiree standing there. He flipped the switch and the lights came back on.

And then he realized that Desiree didn't know who was here.

At this point, he was so tired and so relieved that nothing bad had happened that he just couldn't care.

Tanner was snickering and he glanced over at him. "I'm just glad we didn't have to defend you and Kendra. I was really worried that something bad was happening."

"Me too," Tucker said. "Now help me get all these people out of the house before they realize who is here."

"It's only Travis, me, and Desiree. The others we told to hang back and let us see what was going on. And besides, you know most of the bunch is not going to answer the call."

With a sigh, he entered the house and saw Kendra standing in the corner watching with frightened wide eyes. "What happened?"

"Eugenia thought we needed some time alone in the dark. She thinks things have been tense between us."

"So no one was attacking us?"

"Nope. Just you and me and the ghost."

A giggle erupted from her. "It's a good thing she's already dead or I'd help you get rid of her."

Lavender filled the room and Eugenia appeared. "Dear, what a dreadful thing to say."

"I'm sorry, but I just lost ten years on my life. Any minute, I expected the bad guys to come busting in shooting," Kendra said. "That wasn't nice."

Eugenia smiled. "But you and Tucker are back on speaking terms now."

"Oh good grief. Wake up. Don't you realize your grandson does not want to be with me?"

"That's not exactly true," Tucker said. "I've sworn to never become entangled with my clients and you're my client."

Kendra walked to him, her eyes blazing with heat. She

reached up and pulled his lips to hers. There, in front of his family, she layered her mouth over his, kissing him like she wanted to claim him right there.

At the sound of snickers, Kendra broke off the kiss, stepped back, and smiled at him. "Oh yeah, I think you do want me, Tucker. Screw your rules. You're fired."

"You can't fire me in my own house," he told her.

"I can fire you anytime I want," she said. "And if that will make it easier on you, you're fired."

Travis was trying so hard not to laugh that Tucker glared at him.

"On that note, I think it's time to go," Travis said.

"Wait a minute," Desiree said, walking in between Tucker and Kendra. "I know who you are. You're—"

Tucker reached over and covered her mouth with his hand.

"And we're going to keep that information quiet. Otherwise, tonight will have been a dress rehearsal for the real attack. You're going back and tell everyone a fuse blew and that there was nothing wrong."

Just then the door opened and they all turned to stare as Aunt Rose walked in. Oh no, not what he needed right now. The woman could be a real pain in the ass.

"What the hell is going on here? I heard a code red on the radio."

It was all Tucker could do to keep from groaning. He didn't need his aunt getting involved.

"And what is Kendra Woods doing in your house?"

"Time to go," Travis said as he, Tanner, and Desiree all but ran out the door.

"Great," Tucker said, thinking they were all a bunch of cowards for ducking out when it was about to get tough.

Eugenia appeared. "Hello, Rose. Are you here to cause problems? Because if you are, I could use some practice with my singing."

"Oh shut up, Eugenia. I'm here to learn why Tucker called code red on the radio. And why this young lady is in his home."

There was no getting out of this mess without telling her the truth. And she was not going to be pleased that one of his clients was hiding out here.

"Kendra, meet Aunt Rose. She runs the Burnett Ranch," he said. And wanted to add she was the meanest, crankiest woman on the spread, but thought better of it.

"Nice to meet you," Kendra said reaching out and shaking her hand. "The property is just beautiful."

"Thank you. Now are you here as a guest or are you and Tucker…"

"Both," Eugenia said.

They both turned and glared at the ghost.

"Oh no," Rose said. "Eugenia, are you involved with this?"

"Doing my job. Keeping the family line continuing."

Tucker had the urge to close his eyes and groan but that would get him nowhere.

"Sit down, Aunt Rose, and I'll explain to you what's going on," he said. Then he glared at Eugenia. "I think you've done enough damage tonight. Maybe it's time for you to seek your eternal rest."

The ghost chuckled. "And miss out on all the fun. Hardly."

Kendra walked into the living room, picked up her Kindle and sank down on the couch.

Knowing that his aunt was not going to be happy, he sat on the couch beside Kendra. Tucker hated lying, but if he told his aunt the truth, they would both be on the next helicopter out of here.

And where could he take Kendra that she would be safe?

"I met Kendra while I was doing some security work for her," he said, knowing his aunt's concern would be for their patrons at the dude ranch.

Here was the safest place for Kendra.

"We started dating and I've been on her security detail."

Kendra looked at him and grinned. Oh crap, what was she going to do? For once, could she just play along? After all, she was an actress.

"She's been working so hard and I decided it would be great for her to come to the ranch and rest. We've been here now for six days."

His aunt's eyes narrowed and she gave him that look that said what a bunch of crock.

"Miss Woods, what do you see in my nephew? Why would a beautiful woman with a career like yours be involved with a man like Tucker."

Oh no, what would Kendra say?

She leaned against him and put her hand on his chest. "I know you're his aunt. But take a look at this man. All these gorgeous muscles, his saucy personality, and he even has a brain to go with this manly physique. What more could a woman want?"

His humiliation was now complete.

His aunt shook her head. "You're an excellent actress. I saw the photos of when Tucker saved you outside the restaurant."

"And it was then and there that I fell in love with him. He saved me and now I can't imagine my life without him."

Staring at them, she slowly rose.

"We wanted some time alone, so that's why we've been hiding out at my house," he said.

Rose's brows seemed to rise to her hairline. "Enjoy your stay, Miss Woods. Tucker, there better be no incidents on this property while she's here. Do you understand me?"

"Incidents?"

"As in people trying to reach her," she said. "I suggest the paparazzi not know she's here."

"Agree," Tucker said, thinking she was referring to the men searching for Kendra. Maybe she hadn't heard everything that was going on.

"And, Tucker, don't ever try to hide something like this from me again. Do you understand?"

"Yes, ma'am," he said, remembering she tried to send Tanner packing when she learned what happened between him and Emily in the kitchen.

"Miss Woods, enjoy your stay," she said. "And, Eugenia, one more incident and I will have you removed."

Eugenia laughed. "You should have listened to me, Rose. I could have helped you and then you wouldn't be such a crabby old woman."

His aunt turned and raised her cane shaking it at her. "Don't tempt me to call the ghost remover. I've put his name in my phone. I'm ready to call him."

"Sleep well, Rose," Eugenia said with a laugh. "Go get your beauty rest."

As soon as she was gone, he turned to Kendra and she glared at him.

"You lied," she said.

"And you did as well," he replied.

"I didn't have a choice," she hissed.

"Sure, we did. If we'd told her the truth, we would be packing up and heading out tonight to who knows where. Is that what you wanted?"

With a sigh, she shook her head. "Your family is crazy."

Tucker laughed. "Agree. Not every family has a matchmaking ghost."

She glanced around. "I'm not going to marry him, Eugenia. That's off the table."

"Yes, dear," the ghost replied. "But you two would have beautiful babies together."

Stunned at the thought of babies, he glanced at Kendra. She was looking at him with the oddest expression on her face.

"Babies, a family, everything I've ever wanted and never

126

thought I could have," she said with a wistful sigh. "I'm still not marrying him, Eugenia."

"Really?" Tucker said, gazing at her. "You don't strike me as the kind of person who would want children."

Kendra shook her head at him and sighed. "It's all I truly wanted in life. That and to sing in the church choir. But once they wouldn't accept Grant, I quit. Now instead of singing for the church, I sing for the world."

Tucker stared at her. "Why haven't you married and had a family."

She laughed. "How many men are willing to be Mr. Woods? Or live with the paparazzi following their every move? There's a price for fame, and you don't realize it until you lose your privacy. And now they want to take my life."

CHAPTER 17

The last few days, cabin fever had grown more and more. She needed a break. This morning, Nicole called her and they immediately switched to a Zoom meeting.

"How are you doing," Nicole asked.

"I'm climbing the walls. I've read the script twice, made so many notes, I've read two books and killed at least two dozen mosquitos who I picture as my stalker. Other than that, I'm doing fine. How about you?"

The blonde-haired woman smiled into the camera. "I'm just so excited to be working with an accomplished actress on this project. You know I tried out for your part. I thought there was a chance I could get it since I'm younger than you."

Younger? There was maybe two years difference in ages between them. Two years. Gazing at Nicole's face, Kendra didn't think she had fewer wrinkles than the woman.

Was this a call to make her feel bad because Kendra was not up to playing fake nice today? After last night, she was ready to take someone down on the mat.

"Did you ask Paul why they didn't choose you for Jennifer's

part? I'm playing a woman who has grown children. So I'm even a little younger than what they wanted."

The woman pursed her pouty lips. "He said I was perfect to play the daughter. So it looks like that's who I'll be playing unless you decide to quit because of your stalker."

Was she trying to find out if Kendra was going to quit?

"Sorry, but I refuse to let a criminal force me into making detrimental life decisions. I'm not quitting. No, we're very close to finding the people behind this little detour."

The woman's eyes widened. "That's wonderful. Who do you think is behind this?"

Did she really think she was going to tell her? Why did this call feel a little strange? Maybe Tucker was right. It was someone at the studio. She knew he'd been talking to Anthony, but they had not included her in their discussions.

"I'm not at liberty to say anything, Tucker tells me I can't talk about any of the investigation."

Maybe that would shut her up. Why had she wanted to talk to Kendra?

"Oh, you hired Tucker Burnett of Burnett Security. I hear he's the best. Plus he's certainly handsome enough," she said with a giggle.

A feeling of unease trickled up Kendra's spine. Why did she get the feeling that this was a phishing call? That Nicole was just trying to learn more about Kendra's stalker.

"I hear he has a big ranch in Texas. Is that where you're hiding?"

Now she was terrified. Tamping down the terror that filled her, she started laughing. "Oh no, he has a safe house he takes clients to. A place that no one knows about," she lied hoping to throw her off.

As soon as she got off the phone she had to speak to Tucker. This conversation was not what she expected.

The woman frowned. "Why don't I call you back and we can work on our lines together."

That would never happen.

"I've got to run. Today is my massage and you know how L.A. traffic is," she said.

"It compares with New York City traffic," she said. "Oops."

The woman's eyes widened and she grinned.

She'd fallen for her trap.

"Don't mention New York City to anyone," she said. "Tucker would be furious with me."

The woman faked her smile and an eerie feeling scurried up Kendra's spine. Could she be behind the attacks on her? But why?

"I won't say a thing," she said. "Take care. We'll talk next week."

The hell they would.

"Bye," Kendra said, and as soon as the call was disconnected, she started yelling. "Tucker."

Nothing. The house was silent.

"Tucker," she said again.

Silence. She jumped up from the kitchen table and ran down the hall to his office. The room was empty. She searched all through the house, discovering he was gone.

Picking up her cell phone, she called him. Nothing. He was supposed to be protecting her, where was he?

Gazing around, she figured he wouldn't be far, but she had to speak to him.

Putting her hair up, she put on his old cowboy hat and shades. Glancing out the door, she made certain no one was around and then she hurried hoping he was up at the recreation center.

She all but ran, she was so eager to find him.

When she reached the rec center, she opened the back door and slipped into the kitchen.

"Hello," a woman said. She was at least six months pregnant and busy working on something that looked like lasagna.

"Are you looking for the main dining room? That's where all the games and programs are held."

"No, I'm looking for Tucker. Have you seen him?"

The woman's mouth dropped open.

"My disguise is not very good, is it?"

"No, you're Kendra Woods," she said. "You must be Tucker's mysterious guest."

Kendra smiled. "I am. Please don't tell anyone I'm here. Tucker is going to be furious with me as it is."

Emily smiled at her. "Here, taste the snickerdoodle cookies I made this morning and tell me what you think. I'll call Tanner and ask him if he's seen Tucker."

The woman pushed a tray of still warm cookies towards Kendra and pulled out her cell phone.

"Is Tucker there with you? Have you seen him?" she asked. In the background, she could hear a man speaking but could not understand what he was saying. "You might want to find him. I have his guest here in the kitchen with me," she said softly.

Removing her hat, she took a stool near a stainless-steel worktable.

"That's right. Yes," Emily said with a laugh.

More words were said and then she frowned and glanced at Kendra.

"Are you all right? Tanner wants to know if there is danger at your house?"

She smiled. "Everything is fine, but I need to talk to Tucker right away."

Emily nodded. "All right. She's here and we're having cookies. I'll see you soon. Love you," she said.

The words threw Kendra off. She'd never heard her parents say those words to each other and yet these two acted like it was normal. Like it came naturally. Like the endearment was said all the time.

"How long have you been married?" Kendra asked. Maybe

they were newlyweds and that's how people acted when they were first married.

"Five months," she said smiling. "Our baby was conceived right where you're sitting."

Stunned, Kendra looked down at the floor. "Oh my goodness. You did it right here in the kitchen?"

The woman smiled. "Tanner has PTSD and he started having an episode. Singing always calms him down, so I started singing to him and then we were on the floor amongst the flour and now here we are."

Smiling, Kendra felt tears well in her eyes. As much as she loved singing, she dreamed of having what Emily and Tanner had. Love and a baby on the way.

"Congratulations. What a beautiful story. One you can tell your baby when he's old enough to laugh about it," she said.

"Yes, we're so excited about this child. And Travis and Samantha are also expecting. Both babies are due about the same time," she said.

Just then the doors from the recreation area burst open and Travis walked in with a beautiful woman who was also pregnant.

"What's wrong?"

Emily seemed startled. "Nothing. Kendra is searching for Tucker."

Travis jumped when he saw her, and another pregnant woman came over to her side.

"Hi, I'm Samantha Burnett. You must be our mystery house guest that we're not supposed to know about."

"Yes," Kendra said shaking her hand. "And you're both expecting. Congratulations."

The door burst open again and this time Tucker stormed in followed by Tanner.

"What the hell are you doing?"

The man was clearly upset.

"Well, look it's my bodyguard," she said. "I've been looking for you. Did you lose your cell phone? After I searched the house, I called and got no answer. Have you checked your messages lately?"

Frowning, Tucker glanced down and scowled. "I forgot to turn my phone off silence."

"Not good, when I need you, cowboy."

Crossing his arms over his fully developed chest that once again stretched a form-fitting T-shirt, he frowned at her.

"You weren't supposed to leave the house."

"Well, my only other choice was to call 911. I didn't think you would want the police coming out to look for you."

Shaking his head, he frowned. "Now that you've met the rest of the family, it's time to go."

"Not until I eat another cookie," she said. "These are delicious."

"I'll pack you up a box of them," Emily said.

A guest knocked on the door and Tucker immediately shielded Kendra. His body came around her, his back blocking anyone from seeing her.

Travis answered the door. "Just a moment and she'll be right out." He turned and faced Emily. "They want to speak to the chef."

"I was at the house, frantically trying to find you," he whispered against her ear.

"No, you weren't. I searched everywhere. You were gone," she whispered back.

"Only for ten minutes. You were on your call with that woman."

"And that's what I wanted to talk to you about. Something isn't right," she said.

Emily walked over to Kendra. "It was nice to meet you. Your secret is safe with me."

"Thank you," Kendra said. "And these cookies are so good."

"Thanks," Emily said and then she walked out the door to the recreation room.

"Come on, let's get you out of here," Tucker said as he picked up her hat and shoved it back on her head. "Nice hat."

Samantha laughed. "No one would believe that was you beneath that hat."

"It was nice to meet you," Kendra said. "Hopefully I'll see you and Emily again before I leave."

Tucker took her by the arm and began to pull her out the door. "We gotta go."

When they stepped outside, there was a golf cart that he put her in and then crawled in beside her.

It took only a couple of minutes to reach the house. When they walked in, he grabbed her cheeks and pulled her mouth to his.

"Damn, woman, you scared the hell out of me," he said before his lips covered hers.

With a sigh, she relaxed against him, feeling his strength beneath her hands. She ripped his T-shirt needing to touch his flesh, feel those hardened muscles with her fingers.

Blood roared in Kendra's ears as she leaned into Tucker's kiss, unable to resist the pull of his attraction any longer. The realization that she cared for this man made her reckless. She was defenseless against her unbearable need to be in his arms. And she could no longer fight the feelings she had for this man.

Consequences be damned, she was hungry for the feel of his body twined around hers, delirious with wanting him, desperate to be possessed by Tucker. His mouth plundered hers, and she returned his feverous kisses with a fierceness that surprised her. She placed her hands on his face and molded his lips to hers, opening to receive him. He tasted of sun-kissed days and pleasure-filled nights. Sweet, sinful sensations erupted in a delicious soft moan that escaped the back of her throat.

Pushing him, her lips still entwined with his, she walked them toward the guest room where she stayed, but he resisted her and pulled her along the hallway to the door to his suite.

"Rules be damned," he said quietly. "Besides, you fired me last night."

With a giggle, she let him lead her to the bed.

"Finally," she said with a sigh. "Finally."

CHAPTER 18

*W*hen Tucker couldn't find Kendra, his heart had almost thumped out of his chest. Fear had him running from one building to another, fearing the worst. What if they kidnapped her? How would he find her?

The thought of her being taken had him panicked until Tanner found him and told him Emily had just called. Kendra was in the kitchen.

How had he forgotten to turn his phone back on?

What kind of dumbass did that?

When he'd seen her sitting in the kitchen calmly talking to Emily, he was done. No more waiting. No more following the rules. He had to have her now.

Screw his rules.

When he got her home and kissed her, she had clawed at his shirt until she'd ripped the material from his body. The time for waiting was over.

Kendra pushed him down the hall to her room, but he wanted to see her naked in his room. He wanted to explore every inch of her luscious body in his big king-size bed. Not those small beds in the guest room. She deserved the best and he was going to do everything in his power to give her that this afternoon.

No one better show up here today. They were going to be occupied and this house just might be knocked off its foundation by the time he was finished with her. They were not coming up for air for hours as far as he was concerned.

As soon as they stepped into his room, her mouth remained on his, her hands running down his chest. He twisted her around and pushed her onto the bed and then he followed her. His mouth consumed hers like a starving man in need of pleasure. He took her hands in his and raised them over her head, pinning her to the bed, while his mouth plundered her full and inviting lips until she was moaning.

Why had he waited so long?

He leaned into her body, pressing against her, needing to feel her breasts against his chest, the touch of her body against his. He left her mouth and nibbled his way down past her ears to her neck.

"Tucker," she moaned. "Hurry."

"Oh no, darling. We're doing this right."

His cock was rock hard as he continued his way down to the swells of her breast. Those tempting orbs that he'd stared at for weeks now. That he'd longed to touch and suck. That he'd dreamed of holding in his hands.

He longed to bury his face in her cleavage and tried to remind himself to slow down. Take deep breaths.

He dropped her wrists, wrapping her face in his hands, and brought her mouth to his again. He pushed his tongue past her lips and caressed her mouth like he was dying of thirst, and she was his fountain of water. Her sweet lips tasted of pleasure, and he sampled her mouth, sweeping his tongue across her full lips.

She pushed him away, her breathing harsh, her eyes wide with wonder.

"Time to get naked, cowboy. You've made me wait long

enough," she said, pushing him to a sitting position. She rose and pulled the shirt she wore over her head.

All he could do was stare as she unsnapped the hook on her bra and dropped the garment over the side of the bed.

Her full breasts were so tempting that he leaned forward to kiss them.

"Oh no," she said. "Your turn."

She didn't have to tell him twice. He pulled off the remnants of his T-shirt and tossed it to the floor.

"Your turn," he told her.

Grinning, she kicked off her sandals and then looked at him expectedly.

"Not fair," he said and pulled off his boots and socks. He was ready to get naked and she had very few clothes left.

"Next," he said and leaned back to watch her remove her yoga pants.

All she had left was a skimpy pair of silk panties that he couldn't wait to rip off her.

"Oh, to hell with this," he said, standing and yanking down his jeans and briefs.

For weeks, they had been playing this game of tempting and teasing, and he was done with it. He wanted her, and now.

With his cock at full attention, he climbed back onto the bed and reached for her, pulling her onto the bed with him.

"Oh, Tucker," she said as she reached down and gripped his manhood. "I knew you would be well muscled."

"Enough talking," he said as he pulled one of her nipples into his mouth.

She was gorgeous, and he reached down between her legs and ripped off the piece of silk that was a barrier to her womanhood. He wanted it all.

Now.

"That's better," he said with a whisper. "Now I can touch you everywhere."

She sighed. "Shut up and get busy. I've been waiting for days to feel you between my legs."

A chuckle escaped him and he wanted to tease her but could not wait any longer.

They came together, flesh against flesh, and he needed her like the earth needed rain. After thinking he'd lost her, he had to have her like this, in his bed, her naked flesh beneath his own. After today, he was in real trouble with his client.

He moved his palm down her body, caressing her silken skin until he found her breasts. The feel of her soft flesh, her nipples tightening beneath his touch, was almost too much to bear. He'd wanted her for what seemed like forever. He'd dreamed of her just like this, lying in his bed, his hands and mouth teasing her body until she cried out his name.

But that had been a dream, and this was reality. A reality where he was breaking his rules, but he didn't care.

No longer were policies important. Only being with Kendra.

He put his mouth to her breasts, savoring their sweet taste. She gasped and arched her back toward him. Her hands grabbed his hair and held his mouth to her hardened kernel.

He skimmed his hand down her body, past her ribs, down her smooth stomach, past her belly button, to her womanly folds. She moaned a deep, throaty purr beneath his touch as he slid his fingers into her moist center.

Teasing her, he found her clitoris and rubbed until she clawed at the sheets.

"Tucker," she moaned as she cried out, sending desire rippling through him.

That beautiful voice that millions of people loved, crying out his name, was music to his ears. That sound told him she was just as enthralled with him as he was with her.

That she wanted him and nothing pleased him more.

He moved his lips over hers, wanting to consume her. God, he loved it when she called out his name like he was the only person she needed and wanted. Like he was the one person in this world she could depend on.

He wanted to give her everything. He wanted to fulfill all her wishes and have those sapphire eyes gaze at him like he was the man she trusted more than anything in this world.

And he would protect her as long as she needed and wanted him. With his last dying breath, he would defend her. Nothing was going to take her from him. Nothing.

She wrapped her fingers around his manhood, but he felt her touch all the way to his heart. No woman had ever made him feel this way, and in some ways, it was frightening. Because he could see himself falling in love with her.

With a gentle grip, she slid her hand up and down his shaft. He wouldn't last long. He couldn't hold off forever. The feel of her fingertips gliding up and down him was rushing him to the edge, pushing him ever closer.

"Wait," he said his voice breathy.

Reaching over, he opened the nightstand drawer and pulled out a condom. Quickly he tore the package open and slid it over his erection.

Then he moved her. Time to take her, claim her, make her his.

With desire-glazed eyes, she smiled at him. "Take me to the moon and back."

"Always, darling," he said with a groan as he spread her legs and glided into her.

Slowly he thrust, filling her, surrounded by the feel of Kendra. He loved the way she moaned as he moved within her.

She opened her eyes, her pupils full and dilated in the light of the afternoon sun. She stared at him, her gaze holding him hostage, her body tormenting his, with Kendra filling his soul. He'd never expected to be like this with the two of them spending the afternoon in the throes of passion. But today, he'd felt the fear of losing her and that frightened him worse than anything.

It had been so long since he'd had a woman, and she filled all the empty places in his heart, and her body molded perfectly to his own. This was where he was meant to be and he'd never dreamed that was possible.

She gripped his shaft with her inner muscles, and he thought he was going to lose it right then. Sweet, sweet friction stroked him, surrounded him, their hips moving in rhythm with fierceness and an intensity that surprised him. He plunged deeper into her, and with every driving movement, she matched him.

This sweet woman was torturing him and he loved every moment.

Burning pleasure encompassed him with each long stroke and swirled him closer to the edge. She met every pounding thrust of him, gripping his erection, consuming him with a wildness that drove him to the extreme.

Passion filled him until he thought he would burst from the feelings Kendra evoked in him. The sensations were so stirring and felt so right; he was shocked at their joining. He'd never experienced these emotions.

He never dreamed it would be anything more than a mere joining of bodies, but it was everything he could ever have wanted.

He reached for her face and brought her mouth to his, devouring her with a hungry kiss that consumed him, holding her lips firmly against his. She shuddered, pulling away from him.

"Tucker," she cried, her body racked with tremors.

As he felt her orgasm rock through him, he relinquished the tightly controlled rein he'd been holding onto as he shuddered his release deep within her.

"Kendra," he cried as the pleasure he'd felt in her arms imprinted onto his soul. He'd never had anything so good. He'd never felt so whole, so complete, and so loved in all of his years.

But did she feel the same?

Slowly, their breathing returned to normal, their naked skin warm against one another's. Kendra didn't say anything, and he rolled them over onto their sides and pulled her up against him, not wanting her far from him. Needing her close.

What had just happened to him? Never before had sex been so gratifying, so emotional, it left him stunned. What had Kendra done to him to make him think of more than just one night together?

She was an actress, a singer, and Hollywood royalty, and he was just a wealthy bodyguard. What would she see in him besides really good sex?

He leaned in and kissed her shoulder, his lips leaving a wet trail all the way to her ear.

She shivered. "Hmm, if you don't stop, I'm going to make you regret that."

Her words challenged him and made him move his lips down her shoulder as far as he could reach. He wanted to flip her onto her back and kiss her luscious breasts. "How? Nothing can make me regret being here with you."

She laughed. "Good. It's been a long time since I've had sex. A very long time. I'm ready to go again. How about you?"

"Not without me," he said, his tongue trailing down her back. "We've got all afternoon. And there are some areas I didn't get to taste yet."

"Oh, Tucker," she said with a sigh. "I thought you would never take me to bed."

"Remember, you fired me," he said. "Now I can do whatever you want."

"You know what I want," she said softly, staring up at him. "Do it again."

CHAPTER 19

*T*hey spent all afternoon and evening in bed. The sex had been absolutely mind-blowing. Better than anything she'd ever experienced. This morning she woke up with Tucker's arms around her, wondering how she could return to her single life.

By unspoken agreement, they had not mentioned the stalker or anything happening outside of the bedroom. They had taken a vacation from life and enjoyed one another.

It was their time together, not to be interrupted by the outside world.

This morning they sat across from each other drinking coffee, both of them gazing at their phones.

It was then that she recalled Nicole.

"Oh, I forgot to tell you the reason I was searching for you," she said, remembering the conversation and shuddering.

"Remember us talking about Nicole Cohen," she said. "She's playing one of Jennifer's friends in the movie I'm in. She had tried out for the lead role, but they gave her the secondary role."

Tucker frowned. "She's the one you had the Zoom call with."

"Yes," she said. "Yesterday, when she called, she was very

inquisitive about where I was. She wanted to know if I was quitting the movie because of my stalker. I told her no that a criminal was not going to force me to quit. She acted weird."

"What else did she say?"

"Oh, she said *I hear you hired Tucker Burnett*. She told me you had a big ranch in Texas and wanted to know if that's where I was hiding."

"Shit," Tucker said.

"I told her that you have a safe house no one knows about. Then when she said she had to go because of traffic, I *accidentally* mentioned it was the same as New York City traffic. And then I said *oops, please don't tell anyone*."

He grinned at her. "Very good."

"That call made me suspicious that either she or the studio is what this is all about," she said. "But why would she try to get me to quit the movie? I don't think the studio would give her the part of Jennifer. It is way too weird for her to be the stalker."

Tucker frowned and she could almost see the wheels whirling in his mind thinking about what she'd told him.

"Anthony is supposed to be contacting me today about the studio. I'm going to do a more thorough search on Miss Cohen. But I fear that if she figured out you're in Texas our stalker will too. I'm going to put on extra security."

She reached across the table and kissed him.

"By the way, you're still fired," she said. "After last night there is only one job for you."

He grinned. "Stay inside today. I'm going up to the house to talk to Tanner and Travis. Don't open the door for anyone."

"Bye," she said and walked into the living area and out onto the outside deck just as the front door closed.

The smell of lavender filled the air.

"What do you want, Eugenia?" she asked still sipping on her coffee. They hadn't gotten much sleep last night and she needed the caffeine to stay awake.

The ghost shimmered into view. "You and Tucker are doing much better. I think my plan is working."

She didn't want to admit to the ghost that things were better and yet she couldn't keep the smile off her face.

"Things are better," she said.

The ghost smiled. "Oh, what a happy day. I'm so thrilled that another of my grandsons will soon be getting married."

A trickle of alarm spiraled down Kendra's spine. Could Tucker handle being called Mr. Woods? Because no matter what, some stupid clown would refer to him that way. Could he handle the paparazzi following their every move?

Would he be willing to risk having children with her and them being raised in the spotlight?

As much as she knew she was falling in love with him, last night there had been no talk of the future. She didn't do one-night stands. And yet part of her feared that her feelings were only because of the extreme stress she'd been under.

And yet last night had been wonderful.

"Dear, you look worried," Eugenia said. "My grandson is falling in love with you. I can tell. There's nothing to be worried about."

Oh, she wished that was true, but frankly, she feared there was so much to be concerned about. Mainly that a stalker still wanted to kill her. Eugenia just didn't understand.

"I wish that was true, Eugenia," she said.

Just then her phone rang and she stared at the number. She didn't recognize it.

"Hello," she said fear gripping her.

"Just checking to see if you were home," the voice said.

Click the phone went dead. "That was weird."

It was her cell phone. How could that tell him that she was home? Unless he was listening for the ringtone.

"Oh no," she said and jumped up. She ran into the house and locked the door to the deck. Then she made certain the front door was locked. They were both secure and she sighed. It was then she heard the click of the hammer of a gun.

"Finally, bitch," the female voice said. "Finally."

Whirling around she stared at Nicole. "How did you get in here?"

She laughed. "I'm an actress. I had a special delivery for chef Emily Burnett. The guard gate let me in because he thought I was delivering the spices she'd ordered. Sadly, her spices should soon be exploding to get everyone's attention in about three minutes."

The woman was pregnant.

The scent of lavender wafted in the air.

"She's pregnant," Kendra cried, hoping her favorite ghost was listening. "Kill me, but please don't harm Emily or her husband. They're expecting their first baby."

A cold smile crossed her face. "I love screwing up people's lives. It gives me so much to work with being an actress. First-hand emotion right there playing out in front of me. A pregnant woman and her baby blown to bits. We get to see her grieving husband deal with the emotions of what he's lost."

What a cold-hearted bitch.

"I get that you want to kill me. Why, I have no idea, but that's fine. Kill me, but leave them alone," she said. "They've done nothing to you. Hell, I don't even know why you hate me."

Nicole's beautiful face squinted. "Your father was a worthless asshole who worked for my uncle. One of his minions, if you get my drift. He worked for the family until he disappeared."

Staring at her, she wondered how she knew about her father's disappearance unless her family got rid of him. Yes, her father was an asshole and he mysteriously vanished right after she graduated high school.

"Believe me, all he left us was bills. Nothing else," she said. "So if you're here for his big inheritance, I'll let you repay me the bills he left. Will that make you feel like you're part of the family?"

Her big emerald eyes narrowed and the gun in her hand shook.

"There's nothing I want from you except the role of Jennifer. That was all I ever wanted and you took that from me."

Kendra felt the urge to put distance between them, so she walked into the living room, wondering what piece of furniture she could either lift and toss at her or would be good at protecting her from a bullet.

"How could I take that role from you? They gave you the role of Crystal," she said.

Still pointing the gun at her, Nicole walked toward Kendra. The smell of lavender had dissipated and Kendra hoped Eugenia had gone after Tucker. Or maybe she was saving Emily and the baby. Please let her be saving Emily.

Could she lead the woman out of the house onto the deck where hopefully someone would see that she was in danger?

"No, my uncle has threatened the studio. They are in agreement that if you are no longer the actress playing Jennifer, I get the part. You refused to heed my warnings, so now you're going to die, bitch."

That made her dislike the studio executives, but then again, how did she know this was true? And did they have any choice if her uncle was threatening them? The woman was crafty.

"You know, if you had just left me alone and done the role of Crystal like they wanted, your career would probably have skyrocketed. As your lead actress, I would have supported you, and the next film you would have gotten the lead. But now, you'll be caught. Now you'll go to jail."

Nicole glanced down at her watch. "Time is almost up. In one minute, I'm going to time the sound of your shot to the blast."

"Why not just use a silencer," Kendra said. "Seems like it would have been easier. And how are you going to get out of here without being seen? This ranch has more cameras than the film studio."

She ignored her comment. "Any last requests?"

"Yes, why are you destroying your life over a role in a movie? And you weren't the one shooting at me from the car," Kendra said, wondering who was helping her.

"No," she said with a smile. "My uncle's associates have been helping me. The *capo* your father often did odd jobs for. Until he double-crossed him and then he disappeared. I wonder what happened to your father."

Capo? That was a powerful person in the mafia. Now the bomb seemed possible. She'd had help. Where was her own help when she needed them? How could she slow down the woman and keep her from shooting her?

"What if your bomb doesn't go off on time? What if you can't get out of here with the army of Burnetts waiting outside for you? You do know that Tucker's brothers are very firearm proficient. You don't stand much of a chance."

She smiled. "No. They are going to be occupied putting out the fire and trying to find Emily's body. I have no worries about my delivery truck rattling out of here. Leaving you dead on the floor. And the role of Jennifer will be mine."

The front door was suddenly kicked in slamming against the wall. Nicole whirled around to shoot whoever was there. Kendra ran at her, afraid she'd shoot Tucker. She would rather die than have the man she loved be killed because of her.

Nicole fired a shot just as Kendra knocked her to the ground, missing him. The gun became trapped between them. Lying on top of her, Kendra wrestled for the gun as Tucker ran to her side.

Nicole smiled that crazy beautiful smile of hers as her finger squeezed the trigger.

The bullet slammed into Kendra's shoulder and threw her across the room.

Tucker screamed. "Kendra."

He grabbed the gun from Nicole and punched her in the face, knocking her out cold.

"Bomb," she muttered lying up against the wall. "Emily. Get Emily out of the kitchen."

"She's safe," Tucker said, rushing to her side.

Blood poured from her wound and he ripped his shirt off, waded it up, and held it against the bullet hole.

"Damn, don't you die on me," he said.

She smiled up at him and reached out and touched his face. Her pulse thundered in her ears.

"Get the helicopter ready to fly," Tucker said into his radio.

Just then Travis came bounding into the room.

"Police are on their way," he said.

"Make certain that bitch is tied up. I knocked her out, but she needs to be in handcuffs before she comes too."

"Tucker," Kendra said, gazing at him as her vision tunneled down to only him. Her head felt light and her body tingly.

"Tucker, I—lo—"

"Kendra, stay with me," Tucker screamed.

But the dark was closing in on her. Her hand fell to her side, just as they lifted her and put her on a stretcher.

The smell of lavender filled the air. "Hang on, you can't die. You saved my grandbaby. Please don't die."

Tucker was beside her and she felt his presence more than saw him.

"Damn it, Kendra. Don't die on me. Please don't die."

CHAPTER 20

*I*t was a wonder he wasn't in jail.

He'd been in the administration building talking to Travis and Tanner about the latest developments in the case. The smell of lavender had filled the room. Thank God, the guests were busy at the pool when Eugenia made her appearance.

"There's a bomb in the kitchen. Emily is in danger," she said and from the frantic tone in her voice, he didn't question how she knew this.

They rushed into the kitchen and sure enough, Emily was just about to open a box of new spices when they stopped her.

Tanner picked up the box and ran it out to the dumpster where it had exploded almost immediately.

That's when Tucker knew Kendra was in danger. He'd run all the way to his house, and when he peeked in the window, he'd seen that Nicole had a gun on Kendra.

A big gun that would kill Kendra.

Not waiting for his brothers, he'd kicked the door in, but the damn fool woman that he was falling in love with charged Nicole.

Over and over, his mind played that scene of Kendra rushing

Nicole and her turning at the last second and the two women fighting for control of the gun. He'd tried to get there before she fired the pistol, but he'd been one second too late.

One second that now had him sitting in a hospital waiting room with his brothers and sisters-in-law waiting to learn Kendra's fate.

She was in surgery.

Anthony was on his way.

The sheriff had already spoken to Tucker. They told him about the bomb but the sheriff was their cousin, Matt Burnett, and when they mentioned Eugenia, he'd raised his brows.

"Now, how am I supposed to put that in a report?" Matt had said.

"I don't know, but it's the truth. She warned us about the bomb in the kitchen. Otherwise, we'd be investigating Emily's death too."

Tanner stood there and gazed at Matt. "Nicole intended to kill my wife and baby to keep us occupied while she killed Kendra. I want that bitch prosecuted to the full extent of the law."

And so did Tucker, but he also wanted to know who was behind this and why Nicole thought she should kill Kendra to get what she wanted. A role in a movie. There had to be more than this to the story.

The police had taken Nicole into custody and were holding her in jail. They were all waiting to see if Kendra was going to live or if the charges would be changed to murder.

Even now, the L.A. police were investigating the studio to see what part they played in Kendra being terrorized.

Tucker paced the hospital waiting room. Grateful to his family for waiting with him, but the ladies were pregnant and this had been a stressful day. Once she came out of surgery, he would call Kendra's sister in Mississippi and tell her what happened. But for now, he paced.

An hour later, the doctor came to the door. "Are you here for Kendra Woods?"

"Yes, sir," he said hoping that he would not give him some kind of bullshit about the HIPPA laws and how he could not tell him anything.

He walked over to the door and the doctor pulled him into a conference room. "I'm telling you this because she has mentioned you over and over. She's asking for you."

His heart clenched. "Is she all right?"

"She's going to make it. The bullet missed the main artery by a fourth of an inch. She would have bled out if it had been any closer."

He'd held his shirt to her shoulder all the way to the hospital. Travis had grabbed him another shirt and that's the only reason he wasn't wearing a blood-soaked shirt.

"She's going to need therapy to learn to use that shoulder again. Miss Woods was very lucky tonight," the doctor said. "You can go back and see her when she comes out of recovery. No one else."

A sigh escaped him and his eyes flooded with tears. Years ago, he lost his roommate for trying to protect him and tonight he'd almost lost Kendra in the same situation. It felt like déjà vu all over again, only this time Kendra was alive.

"Thank you, Doctor," he said, his heart almost splintering. He could not live through losing someone he loved again. No, he hadn't loved Brent, but they were good friends.

"Miss Woods is a celebrity. We're putting her on strict lockdown and my staff has been given instructions that if they say she's here, they will lose their jobs."

That was a warning to him that it was going to be hard to keep this quiet. "Look, she was almost killed tonight and while I think we've captured her killer, one of my men or myself will be stationed outside her door. No one gets in to see her except myself and Anthony Emanuel, her agent. In the morning, I'll give the administrator a list of who she can see."

The man nodded. "Good idea."

"I'm leaving for the night. The nurses know to call me if anything should go wrong."

"Thank you," Tucker said, wiping the tears from his eyes.

After the doctor left, he sat in the room a little longer thinking about how Nicole had gotten through their defenses. Could someone do that here in the hospital as well? She couldn't be the only one behind this.

There had to be more.

Finally he stood and walked out of the room, more determined than ever not to let her be alone. He'd failed as her protector, but he would not let whoever finish the job.

His family stood around with anxious eyes staring at him.

"Is she all right?" Emily asked.

"The doctor thinks she's going to make it. She'll need therapy to relearn how to use that arm. A quarter inch closer and the bullet would have hit the main artery. She would have bled out."

Suddenly his family surrounded him, hugging him close. They had never done that before and it brought tears to his eyes. His sisters-in-law were the best and they knew that Kendra had been worried about Emily and the baby.

"I know you're staying. Do you need me to bring you anything?" Travis asked.

"Yes," Tucker said. "My laptop. I need to do more research on Nicole. She cannot be the only person behind this. My gut instinct is warning me there are more."

Tanner nodded. "I'll come back and relieve you whenever you want me to. Just tell me when."

That was a really great offer from his brother who had PTSD. But he'd handled the bomb with no episode, even though it had been dangerous.

"Thank you, for getting rid of that bomb," Tucker said. "That showed real courage."

"Courage, hell, that was my wife and baby in the kitchen."

Emily put her arm around him. "His PTSD is so much better since we've been together. I think soon it will be in his past."

Travis wrapped his arm around his wife, Samantha. "We need to get the women home. But I want you to know that I'm having a meeting in the morning with the staff. Nicole getting through the gate as a delivery driver was not good. That needs to be addressed."

"Agree," Tucker said. "What the stupid girl didn't know is that I have cameras with audio set up through the house and it's all recorded. I'm going to copy it and turn it over to the sheriff."

In some ways, he couldn't wait to get his hands on that footage. It would tell him so much about Nicole and her motive.

But he couldn't leave Kendra. Not when she was at her most vulnerable. Not now.

"Thank you, guys, for coming to the hospital," he said. "It means so much."

Samantha waddled up to him. "Tucker, just admit you're falling in love with her. We can see it plainly. And we're happy for you."

Emily laughed. "Eugenia has struck again. But I would never have thought it would be with a celebrity. She's nice, Tucker, and if you love her, then I know she's the right person for you. Already we love her because you do."

Those damn pesky tears welled in his eyes and he had to look away. Though he had yet to say the words to Kendra, he knew where his heart was. But that frightened him. Loving Kendra would not be an easy life.

Between the paparazzi, the crazies, and her lifestyle, it would be difficult.

"Thank you," he said, hugging Emily and Samantha and then

he glanced at his brothers. "Take your wives home before they have me crying like a big ole soft teddy bear."

They all laughed.

"Good night, Tucker," Emily called.

He watched them disappear down the hospital hallway and shook his head. How in the hell had he gotten so damn lucky to have a family who looked out for each other?

A nurse came down the hallway.

"Mr. Burnett, Miss Woods is in her room. She's asking for you," she said.

He followed the nurse down the hall, anxious to see the woman who had captured his heart. But could he marry her?

When they walked into the room, she had an IV dripping in her arm and a pain pump. He could see she was going in and out. He walked to the side of her bed and picked up her hand.

Immediately she opened her eyes and then she tried to smile. "Hi."

"Hi," he said.

"I thought I fired you," she said.

"You did. But I didn't follow your orders," he replied, his heart clenching. But he'd done a lousy job. Because of his failure, here she was in a hospital bed with a bullet hole in her shoulder.

"I'm glad," she said. "Is everyone okay?"

"Everyone but you is fine. You, I'm worried about. I'm not leaving your side," he told her.

She smiled. "Good. Call my sister before she hears about this on the news."

"I will," he said. "You go to sleep. I'll be right here sleeping in this chair beside you."

"I'd rather you crawled up in bed with me," she said.

He laughed. "Me too, but I don't think your nurse or your doctor would appreciate me being in your bed."

"Probably not," she said as the pain meds kicked in and she drifted off.

He pulled up the chair next to her bed and sank down in it. He'd failed her. Failed her badly, and he was angry as he went over everything in his mind once again. What had he missed?

After the nurse left the room, he checked his gun. He checked his phone and then he glanced around the hospital room, planning how he could protect her if they were attacked here.

When the nurse came back to check her vitals, he glanced at her badge. It had her name, photo, and, of course, the hospital's name on it.

With a sigh, he knew it was going to be an intense few days, and as much as he wanted to sleep, he couldn't. Finally, right before dawn, he dozed off.

Two hours later, Travis walked in.

"Wake up," he said. "We've got to talk."

"I brought you your laptop and the film from the shooting," Travis said. "There is some new information, plus, I made a list of everyone who could be a possible suspect."

Tucker sat up and yawned. He glanced at Kendra; she'd slept through the night. Her eyes opened and she glanced around.

"Where am I?"

"You're in a hospital, sweetheart," he said. She didn't remember them talking last night?

Just then the doctor walked in. He glanced over at Travis. "What's he doing in here?"

"He's my brother and he's brought me my laptop and information about the case," Tucker said.

The doctor nodded. "Why don't both of you step out, while I examine my patient."

Tucker didn't want to go anywhere, but he glanced at Kendra. Picking up her hand, he squeezed it. "I'll be right on the other side of the door."

She nodded.

Walking outside with his brother, he gazed at him. "Thanks for bringing my laptop. You watched the video?"

"Yes, Nicole's uncle is the head of the Lucchese family. Thank goodness your security video has sound and not just video."

Tucker tried to remember what Kendra had said about their father. Only that he was a jerk. He should call her sister later today and speak to her.

"What else did you learn?"

"Nicole wanted her role in the movie," he said.

For the next five minutes, they discussed everything he'd learned on the recording. Tucker wanted to watch it himself, but replaying it in Kendra's room was probably not a good idea.

The doctor walked out.

"She's doing great. I expect her to be here in the hospital for about two more days before we send her home. And even then, she's going to need rest for at least two weeks before she can start back doing her normal routine. I'll also set up a physical therapist for her before she leaves the hospital."

"Thanks, Doctor," he told him. It was then he saw Anthony walking down the hall toward him.

"I've got news," he said. "Not good either."

CHAPTER 21

*A*fter Kendra spoke to the doctor, the nurse came in and gave her some pills. Lying in the bed, she tried to remember everything that happened yesterday. The bullet wound and loss of blood had made her memory fuzzy and she didn't want to forget.

No, she needed to remember for when she spoke to the police about what Nicole had done to her.

From the time Nicole arrived until they were carrying her out of the house on a stretcher, had only been minutes, though it felt like forever.

It all seemed surreal and she felt lucky to be alive.

But what had they done to Nicole? Where was she?

She wondered where her cell phone was. She wanted to call her sister and talk to her about what Nicole had told her.

Yes, her father had been a drunk who worked nefarious shady jobs, but had he worked for the mob? Though she never said it, Nicole's uncle worked for the mob.

Her mind swirled, and then suddenly, she grew tired and drifted off to sleep. Her body demanded she rest. The sound of the door moving had her opening her eyes, her heart pounding.

If Nicole was in custody, why did she feel so jumpy? Or would she always feel this way now?

Anthony walked in and her eyes teared up. Oh, how she loved this man who had guided her career for so long.

He came to her bedside and took her hand.

"How's my favorite troublemaking star?"

For some reason, she felt so weepy today. "Shaken."

All her life, she'd been the strong one, the person who wasn't afraid, but staring down a gun barrel did things to you. Made you realize the fragileness of life. They could have been planning her funeral today.

"I'm staying with you while Tucker runs home and takes a shower. Travis, his brother, is here with me and one of the men from Burnett Security is on his way."

If they had Nicole in custody, why were they making certain she wasn't alone?

"What about the studio? Have you talked to them?"

Anthony didn't say anything. "The picture is on hold for now."

"No, it's not," she said, suddenly feeling defiant. "That is a great movie and I'll be damned if my little problem with my coworker is going to keep me from making this film."

It was the first time she felt like her old self since before the attack. Just the thought of this picture being stopped made her angry.

"There's more to it than that," Anthony said. "But don't worry, I'm already looking for a new project."

Staring at him, he didn't seem like his chipper self. She could see the emotion on his face, and his eyes appeared teary.

"No, I want to do *that* movie," she said. "What's the problem? You're not telling me everything."

He walked around the bed to the side where her IV pole stood with the line going into her arm.

There was a knock on the door. Travis lugged in a huge

SYLVIA MCDANIEL

bouquet of flowers. He handed her the card and she glanced down at the message.

Get well. We can't wait to start this film with you as our star. Paul Shell and Shadow Works Studios

Travis brought them in. He glanced at Anthony. "They've been searched."

Why were they searching her flowers if they had stopped production?

Anthony nodded.

Tucker sat the flowers down and walked out the door. The message on the card and what Anthony was telling her didn't match. Something was off. Way off.

"Kendra, you know I check every studio out. I verify all the information in your contracts before I even bring them to you. My lawyer that is on staff reads and verifies everything," he said. "I would never have you agree to work with a studio that I thought was crooked."

Sitting up, she stared at Anthony. He seemed nervous. Almost frightened.

"What's wrong?"

He glanced down at his feet and then back up at her. "Nicole's uncle owns most of the studio's stock. He's insisting that you be fired and Nicole be put in your role."

She started laughing until her shoulder began to hurt. "That's going to be kind of hard to do from jail. Because no, this bitch is not going to get away with this."

Anthony looked away and then she noticed tears well in his eyes.

"Is this why she's been terrorizing me? Why did they hire me as the lead actress if her uncle wanted her to be the star?"

But the card said something different.

"The stock has only recently been acquired," he said. "Before today, he didn't have enough votes to take over. He's a very ques-

160

tionable man with ties to the mob. Already the executives are agreeing to his demands."

None of this seemed real. None of it made any sense. A weak moment came over her. There were times when all she wanted to do was close her eyes and sleep.

"All this time, someone has been trying to kill me because they wanted their niece to have the lead role in this movie. That's crazy," she said, fighting drowsiness.

Anthony nodded. "Sadly, Tucker doesn't think it's over. He suspects someone else is behind Nicole's attempt at killing you. And he's right."

She frowned at him. How did he know Tucker was right?

"What do you mean."

From his pocket, he pulled a syringe and held it up to the light. "They're threatening me."

Terror gripped her.

"Anthony. You're making me nervous. What are you doing?" She could see he was distressed.

"What I have to," he said softly.

Her heart stopped. The man she thought of as more like a father than an agent was holding a hypodermic filled with what? Something that would kill her? Why?

"Don't, Anthony," she said,. "You're my friend."

"They didn't give me any choice," he said. "It's you or my daughter. I love Kathleen. She's my only child."

Crying, he tapped the needle, getting ready to put it in her intravenous line.

Picking up her hospital tray, she threw it at him. The tray crashed to the floor. Didn't the guards outside hear the noise?

"Please, don't make it any harder than it already is," he said, tears racing down his cheeks.

She opened her mouth to scream and his hand slapped over her mouth. She reached to yank the IV out of her arm, but he gripped her hand.

"You have to die or else they will kill my daughter," he told her, sobbing.

She couldn't move as she watched the needle come closer and closer to the tube going into her vein. He held her good arm and her bad arm she was unable to use.

The door slammed open and Tucker rushed through.

"Damn it, Anthony, back off. Don't make me kill you," he told him, his Luger pulled out.

"She has to die," he mumbled. "You can't stop me or they will kill my daughter."

"No one is going to die," Tucker said. "Drop the needle now and step away from the bed or I will shoot you."

"You can't fire your weapon because of the oxygen," he said. "That would kill us all. Let me do this so I can save my daughter."

Tucker stepped farther into the room with Travis following him, his gun pointed at Anthony. Jumping on him, he yanked the needle from the man's hands.

Anthony collapsed onto the bed and Kendra wanted to punch him, but she couldn't.

"As soon as I left here, I knew something was wrong. You lied, Anthony. I called the head of the studio and he confirmed your lies. William Lucchese did not purchase the studio's stock."

Kendra sank back into the bed, crying, as she watched Tucker handcuff Anthony. Travis took him away from Tucker.

"I'm sorry, Kendra," Anthony said as they pulled him out the door. "They forced me."

Even so, she would never trust him again.

Tucker sighed and came to her bedside.

"That's three times you've saved my life, cowboy," she said with a sniffle.

"Oh, honey, I'd take you in my arms and hold you, but I can't with your shoulder the way it is," he said, brushing the hair away from her face. "But this time, I can promise you that it's over."

"Really?"

"Yes, really. Nicole Lucchese Cohen is the niece of mobster William Lucchese. She was determined to get your role in the movie. And her uncle was going to do everything he could to help her. They have been working with Anthony since the very first letters. The plan was to force you into quitting, so Nicole could get the part. Now they're all going to jail for a long time."

She sighed. "No more threatening letters?"

"No," he said.

"No more someone doing a drive by and shooting at me?"

"No," Tucker said, feeling certain that once he spoke to Mr. Lucchese, his family would never bother her again. Because she had Burnett Security protecting her. And anyone who touched Kendra would be a dead man.

"No more facing someone with a gun in their hand trying to kill me."

"Definitely no."

"Good," she said. "But you're still fired."

"That's only because you want to have sex with me," he whispered staring into her eyes.

A smile spread across her face.

"Definitely, but not today," she told him. "I think I'm going to need a few days."

The doctor walked in the door and Tucker rose. "Miss Woods, your presence in our hospital has caused quite the stir."

"Yes, Doctor, and I'm sorry. But hopefully after today, it will be just me and Tucker," she said softly, wiping her tears. "When someone is determined to kill you, it's difficult."

The doctor's brows raised. "I'll say. The press is outside the hospital and the CEO would like to make a statement to see if that will appease them and they will go away."

"Tell them that Miss Woods is recovering from a very trying time during which someone tried to kill her. But Burnett Security saved me and as soon as I recover, I will start working on my new project I'm so excited to be a part of."

The doctor frowned and glanced at Tucker. "One more incident in this hospital and you'll be looking for another place to care for Miss Woods."

Tucker grinned at the doctor. "We just foiled an attempted murder on Miss Woods. We now know everyone who was involved, so she should be safe from here on out. But just to make certain, my security team will have someone right outside her door at all times."

The doctor nodded and she heard her cell phone ringing.

As exhausted as she felt, she needed to see who was calling.

"Hand me my phone," she said.

Tucker gave it to her. It was the studio.

"Miss Woods, are you all right?"

It was the head of the studio.

"Yes, sir. I need some answers from you. Would you confirm for me that Mr. Lucchese does not have stock in the studio and that Nicole Cohen is no longer involved with the film? It would be very hard to work with someone who tried to kill me."

The man sighed. "She's been fired. While Mr. Lucchese tried to buy enough stock to control the studio, that was blocked by the SEC. The mob is not going to run this studio as long as there is breath in my body and I'm the head."

She smiled. "Thank you. That makes me feel so much better. Sadly, I will be searching for another agent, but as soon as this bullet hole heals, I'll be ready to start work."

There was a moment of silence on the phone. "I'm so glad to hear that. I feared after everything that had happened, you would back out of the contract. Rest and get well, Miss Woods. We're looking forward to starting production."

"Thank you," she said and disconnected the phone. She gazed at Tucker and could feel her body sinking. "The studio is safe. I'm safe."

The doctor's frown aimed at her. "You need rest."

"Agreed," she said.

Tucker sat in the chair and pulled out his laptop. "I'll be right here."

The doctor eased out the door and the walls of darkness closed in.

With a sigh, she felt her eyelids close. How did a musician/actress and a security man have a relationship? She'd never had anyone by her side while she'd been famous.

Could she do it now?

CHAPTER 22

*I*t was over. Tucker sat in Kendra's hospital room watching her sleep as he finished his reports and filed everything with the local police.

Then he learned where mobster William Lucchese was being held. He would pay the man a visit in jail and promise him that if he harmed Anthony's daughter or Kendra, a price would be paid.

There would be no need to spell it out or say what would happen, but if the man was smart, he would understand. Eye for an eye.

Just as he was about to shut down his computer, he noticed an email he'd not seen.

It was from his past roommate Michael's mother.

He read the note and his heart sank. He'd forgotten that the day after tomorrow was the anniversary of his death. Damn. Normally, he went to visit the cemetery with his parents.

Sadness gripped him and he glanced at the hospital bed where Kendra slept. What was he doing?

Michael's family always expected him on the anniversary of his death. He had to go. And yet, he hated leaving Kendra.

He would not return for several days. Several days of leaving her alone.

But how could he not be with Michael's family?

With a sigh, he leaned down and kissed her on the cheek. Part of him wanted to wake her and explain to her where he was going and why, but she was sleeping so peacefully.

Stepping outside, he glanced around. Travis had left. Everyone except for the man he trusted to guard her had gone.

Going back inside, he picked up her cell phone and dialed her sister's number.

"Are you all right?" her sister asked answering the phone.

"It's Tucker," he said. "I've got to leave her for a few days. I was wondering if you'd like to visit her."

The woman cried out. "Yes. I'm Nancy, by the way."

"Nice to meet you. I'm sending the company jet to pick you up. Pack a bag and be ready to go in four hours," he told her. "As long as she's in the hospital, we'll have a security detail outside her room. She's doing all right, but today was a tough day. Anthony is no longer her agent."

Her sister gasped. "He's been with her since the beginning."

"I'll let her tell you what happened. If I didn't believe she was safe, I wouldn't be leaving," he told her sister. "She doesn't know you're coming, so that will be a wonderful surprise for her."

There was a moment of silence on the phone. "Thank you, Tucker. It must be really important for you to be leaving."

"It is," he said. He'd never forgotten the anniversary of Michael's death, and he couldn't this year either. Even now, sadness overwhelmed him as he thought of his friend who died for him.

"I should be back in a couple of days," he said. "Right now, she's sleeping so peacefully, so she doesn't know I'm leaving."

"Oh no," Nancy said.

"I'll call her later when I can talk to her."

There was so much he and Kendra needed to talk about. As

much as he loved her, did he want her in his life? Could he handle all the press and being part of her entourage?

Did he want to have a family with a woman who couldn't buy new underwear without the world knowing what kind?

"Thanks for coming," he said. "I know this will make her so happy."

And he wanted to do something to give her pleasure. After everything she'd gone through, she deserved some happiness.

"I hope I get to meet you in person," she said. "Again, thanks, Tucker."

He hung up the phone and glanced at the bed where Kendra slept so soundly.

Leaning down, he kissed her on the cheek. "I'll be back, love."

CHAPTER 23

A couple of hours later, Kendra woke in an empty hospital room. Tucker promised her he would be sitting right there in that chair when she awoke. And he was gone.

She'd slept so hard. And this evening, she felt better than she had since the surgery. But where was Tucker?

The nurse nudged open the door gently. "You're awake."

"Yes," she said.

"I came in and took your blood pressure and you slept right through it," she said.

"Is Tucker outside," she asked.

"No, I don't think so," the woman in white said as she took her blood pressure and checked her for fever. "You keep doing this well and we'll be kicking you out of here."

But where was Tucker?

As the woman started toward the door, she called to her. "Would you send in the man standing outside the door?"

"Of course," she said.

A man with a gun on his hip stepped inside. "Do you need something, Miss Woods?"

"Where is Tucker?"

The man frowned. "He had to leave. He said to give you this."

The man pulled out a note in a sealed envelope and handed it to her.

"Thank you," she said.

He left the room and returned to standing outside her door.

Dear Kendra,

I'm sorry, but I had to leave for a few days. You're safe. My men will be guarding the door and no one is going to hurt you. When I return, we'll take you back to your home.

We have much to talk about.

Tucker

She stared at the note. What could be more important than being here with her during this difficult time? Didn't he realize how frightened she remained? Didn't he know she was facing the most difficult decisions she'd ever experienced and he'd deserted her?

Where the hell was he?

She picked up her phone and dialed his number. It went to voice mail.

The door swung open and her sister walked in. Her heart swelled with love and happiness. She'd felt so alone.

"Nancy," she cried as the woman ran to her bedside.

"What are you doing here?"

"Tucker arranged for me to fly here," she said. "He told me he had to leave for several days and he didn't want you to be alone. So I'm your new nursemaid."

Her sister gave her an abbreviated hug.

Tears filled Kendra's eyes. "I'm so happy to see you. Are the kids with you?"

"No, it's just you and me for the next week," she said.

"Oh, Nancy, I've gained and lost so much during this time," she said. "I've fallen in love and lost my agent. Everything is just so messed up."

"Who did you fall in love with?" she asked.

"Tucker, I've fallen in love with my security guy, and yet he disappeared. I don't know where he is or what he's doing. I'm so afraid."

Her sister squeezed her hand and pulled the chair up to the bed. "He called me and asked me to come be with you. He didn't want to leave you alone. That's the sign of a very caring man."

"Why wouldn't he tell me where he's gone," she asked.

"I don't know, but let's give him the benefit of the doubt," she said. "Right now, I think we need to concentrate on you healing and getting your strength back."

"I'm so glad you're here," Kendra said. "Thank you for coming."

"I thought I was going to have to knock down that big burly guy standing at the door. He took out his phone and looked at my picture. Your security man is taking good care of you."

That was what made this so suspicious. Where was Tucker?

CHAPTER 24

Three days later, the helicopter landed at the ranch and he walked down the steps to the waiting car.

For the last three days, he'd been involved with different ceremonies both private and public on the campus of the university, remembering the students who had been killed that fateful day. That day that convinced him, he would go into security and help people, corporations, and even celebrities protect themselves from the crazies in the world.

And strangely enough, he had a calling for it. But now, he wanted to see Kendra. He needed to see her.

The security detail had kept him up to date. He'd tried calling her three different times and each time her cell phone was busy.

That worried him, but he knew she was safe.

Tanner was sitting in the truck waiting for him.

"Welcome back, brother. Do you want the good news or the bad news first?"

Turning he gazed at his brother. "What's happened."

"Oh, nothing much. Kendra was released from the hospital today and she took a private jet back to Hollywood."

"Shit," he said. "I'm going to kick someone's ass for not letting me know this. Someone's head is going to roll."

Tanner chuckled. "Oh, believe me, your security men tried to stop her, but it was no use. She was going home."

How could he blame her? She'd been away for so long and she'd faced so much. But that also probably meant that she was pissed as hell and that was the reason she wasn't returning his calls.

"What else?"

"Aunt Rose is plenty upset about what happened at your house with the gunshots and the police and the paparazzi and the rescue helicopter. She wants to see you now. I'm to take you straight to her office."

"Great," he said. "I'm tired. I've been through an emotional few days and yet I've got to deal with an old woman's fears of how we're ruining the ranch."

Tanner laughed. "It's your turn, brother. All I did was have sex in the kitchen. You, on the other hand, had a gun battle in your home."

The truck pulled up in front of the office and he could see her light on upstairs in her office. A groan came from between his lips.

"I'm going to catch hell, aren't I," he said.

"Yes, you are," Tanner said. "Do you want me to wait or leave you the truck?"

"No, you go on home. If I still have a home, I'll walk there."

Tanner laughed. "Emily said to tell you that she left some leftovers in your fridge. She knew you'd be late getting home."

"You married a sweet woman," Tucker said. "Tell her thank you."

Tanner grinned as Tucker got out of the truck. "So when are you going to ask Kendra to marry you?"

For a moment, Tucker closed his eyes. "I think she's angry with me and she has good reason. I haven't spoken to her since

173

the day Anthony tried to kill her. Michael's parents contacted me and reminded me that this was the anniversary. In order to make it, I had to leave immediately and she was sound asleep."

Tanner shook his head. "Oh man, that was dumb. You're going to have to do something to make it up to her."

But what?

He'd brought in her sister, so they could spend some time together while he was gone and Kendra was in the hospital. But he hadn't expected her to get out quite so quickly. And he had planned on bringing her home to his house. But those plans had gone afoul.

"The bad thing is I'm so damn crazy about her, I can't think straight. And now she's not taking my phone calls."

"I saw the ceremony on television," Tanner said. "Don't you think she saw that and knew where you were?"

You would think, it was all over the news, but then why wouldn't she return his calls?

"I don't know," he said. "First, I have to do damage control here."

"Good luck," Tanner said. "You'll figure out something with Kendra. Emily and I can see that you were meant for one another."

"Thanks," Tucker said. "Right now, I'm not so certain."

He shut the truck door and glanced up at the light in the window. Time for his reckoning.

As he walked into the office, he took the stairs two at a time, hurrying to get this over with so he could rest and relax and try Kendra once again. Plus, he planned on finding out who was on duty the day she was released from the hospital and can his ass.

Then he would find out if his men were still watching the house in Hollywood. Yes, the threat was over, but he still wanted her to have protection.

On the second floor, he knocked on the door to his Aunt Rose's office.

"Come in," she said.

When he walked in, she glared at him. "You have broken more rules than any other Burnett on this ranch."

"How? If you recall, the man in the guard house was the one who let in Nicole. All I did was harbor my client in my house. My client who may soon be my wife. My client who was injured in the attack. If the security guard, who I don't have any control over, had done his job, this would never have occurred. If Miss Woods likes, she could sue us because of that guard."

His aunt licked her lips and sighed. Always go in on attack mode and catch them unawares. He'd learned that long ago. Now he could see his aunt reconsidering.

"How is she?"

"She was released from the hospital today, and I don't know because she's not returning my calls. As soon as I get home, I'm going to try again."

His aunt frowned.

"I saw you on television for the anniversary," she said, changing the subject.

"Yes," he said. "I just got home from there."

Just then, the air filled with the smell of lavender and his aunt groaned. "Go away, Eugenia. We're having a business meeting."

The ghost appeared not far from his aunt.

"How is Kendra? I'm so concerned about her."

"She's doing well," he said. "But she went home to California."

"What?" the ghost said. "Get on that fancy silver bird thing you get on and go find her. She's your wife."

He gave a chuckle. "You want me to marry an actress? A Hollywood legend?"

"Fiddledeedee. I don't care if she's the star of Vaudeville. She's your chosen one and you need to go to her and confess your love."

Staring at the ghost, he started to laugh.

"How are you so certain I love her?"

"Oh, I know. One night there was a lot of noise coming from your bedroom," she said. "I heard things your grandmother should never hear."

Tucker stared at the ghost stunned. "You were in the bedroom?"

"Oh no, I just popped in to see if I could push you two together somehow and there was no need. The bedroom door was closed and there was a banging against the wall and the sound—"

"All right," Tucker said, cutting her off and gazing at Aunt Rose who was trying not to laugh. "If I ever learn you were watching us, I'll have that ghost remover out here before you can apologize."

The ghost giggled. "Oh no, I don't want to see anything. But I know that babies are being created and that makes me so happy."

Babies? They had used a condom, but he wasn't about to tell her that.

"Go to her," the ghost said. "Work out your differences and return to the ranch."

His aunt smiled at him. "Tell her because of the trouble caused at our ranch that I think it would be wonderful if she did a concert here at Christmas. We could call the television special, A Burnett Family Christmas. Do it like the Andy Williams show."

"Who?"

"Oh, you're too young to remember. Look it up on the internet."

"So am I free to go home?"

"No," Eugenia said. "Get on that bird thing and go to California."

As much as he'd like to, he was too tired.

"Tomorrow," he said. "First, I want to try to call her."

What if the reason she wasn't answering was that something had happened? No, he'd caught the bad guys and brought them to justice. She was safe.

But what if she wasn't?

A curse slipped from between his lips.

His aunt glared at him.

"What if she's in danger again? I've got to call her and then I'll leave."

Eugenia started twirling around in the office.

"Bring her home, Tucker, where she belongs," Aunt Rose said as he stood and started for the door.

Already he was pulling out his cell phone and dialing Kendra's number.

Nothing. Absolutely nothing.

He called the number for the Burnett Security team at her house. Judd answered the phone.

"Burnett Security," he said.

"Where is she?" he asked. "She's not answering her phone."

"Uh, boss, where are you? We've been trying to reach you," Judd said. "She's in her house and she's not answering her phone. The paparazzi have been trying to get in and they have her phone number."

Anthony. That son of a bitch must have given them her phone number, knowing they would drive her crazy.

"Don't tell her, but I'm on my way," he said.

"Uh, sir, we've been given orders not to let you in," Judd said.

"And who signs your paycheck," he asked.

"You do," Judd said.

"And are you going to let me in?"

"Of course," Judd said. "But I wanted to warn you that things are not going to be easy."

"Don't worry. I think I know how to fix that," he said.

"She told us that she fired you and we're now her security team."

"And who signs your paychecks?" he asked again.

"You do, sir," he repeated. "By the way, Quinn is back at work today."

Tucker had rehired his worker as soon as he could and the man had been grateful for a second chance. He still warned him away from getting involved, but how could he fire someone when he'd fallen in love with his client?

"See you soon."

he trip home left Kendra exhausted. Maybe she should have followed the doctor's orders and returned to the Burnett ranch for a few days. But there she would have to face Tucker and she was so angry at him, she couldn't stay at his house.

Here she was safely tucked inside her home, though there was quite a bit of damage that needed repair.

Right now, she just wanted to enjoy spending time with her sister and healing. The swelling in her arm had gone down, but it was still black and blue with ten stitches across it.

Taking a shower had been challenging, but now she lay relaxing on the sofa, resting. Nancy was upstairs talking to her family. In a few days, Nancy would go home, but for now, she remained here with Kendra.

And it was so good to see her. They had talked about their father and mother and growing up so dirt poor, it was ridiculous.

Though she knew the security men were Tucker's outfit, as soon as she could, she would find someone to replace them. After all, if he could leave her alone in a hospital with no explanation, then they were done.

About a day ago, her phone started blowing up and she realized someone had leaked her personal phone number to the paparazzi. So she'd turned it off. Maybe Tucker had tried to call, but right now, her heart was breaking.

How could he leave her?

Flipping on the television, the ten o'clock news was coming on. Half gazing at the channel, she watched the news as she flipped through a magazine.

"Texas college held a ten-year ceremony to honor the dead and wounded at the shooting that occurred a decade ago."

Tucker was involved in a school shooting. Her eyes jerked up to the television and she saw him standing dressed in a suit beside a couple. There were families all around, and as each name was called, they walked up and put a wreath on a wooden cross that had the picture of their loved one.

Stunned, she watched him. Grabbing her phone, she quickly turned it on and dialed his number. It went straight to voice mail.

Damn it.

He'd gone to honor his college roommate who had died taking a bullet that was meant for Tucker. She now remembered him telling her that.

How could she be angry with him?

Her sister came into the room. "What's wrong?"

"Look," she said and pushed the button that wound the story backward. "That's Tucker. He was attending the anniversary ceremony for the death of his roommate."

"That's him? He was there at that shooting?"

"Yes, his college roommate took a bullet that was meant for him. It's why he got into security," she said and realized she had not trusted him even though he'd protected her and saved her life not once, but three times.

The doorbell rang, and her sister glanced at her. "Where are the security men?"

Kendra knew.

Instinctively, she jumped up from the couch and went to the door.

"Wait a minute," her sister said.

"No," she replied. "It's Tucker."

She swung open the door and he took her in his arms.

"We need to talk," he said.

"I know where you were," she told him, wrapping one arm around him. "I understand why you left me."

Leaning back in her embrace, he stared at her. "We still need to talk."

Her sister disappeared and she led him into the living room, holding onto his hand. Sinking onto the couch, he faced her.

"Kendra, you started out as my client, but over the days and weeks, I've fallen in love with you. I'm not certain how our life will be with you being a big celebrity, but you'll never have to worry about protection ever again. It's not going to be easy, but if you'll have me, I want to get married. Have babies and raise a family. I'll even stay home and raise the kids while you go do your acting, but most of all I want you."

Tears welled in her eyes and she reached out with her good hand and stroked his face. "No, it's not going to be easy, but I want you by my side. Protecting me and our family. I love you, Tucker Burnett, and I can't wait to become Mrs. Tucker Burnett."

"God, I want to hug you so bad, but I can't," he said, his head coming to her forehead. "I love you so much, Kendra. Somehow we'll make this work. Somehow."

She giggled. "Can we get married at the Burnett Ranch?"

He grinned. "I think that can be arranged as long as you'll do a Christmas special there for Aunt Rose."

"Oh, a Christmas wedding," she said. "That would give me time to create a television special that could end with us getting married."

"If that's what you want, then that's what we'll do," he said. "Only problem…Eugenia."

She giggled. "I love your family. They're so interesting."

CHAPTER 26

*T*ucker watched as his wife in her white dress sang the last song of the evening. His family had all gathered to celebrate the Christmas show and their wedding. As soon as the show was over, they would immediately be getting married.

Gazing at Kendra, he thought she'd never looked more beautiful. The movie *Secrets of a Summer Place* was well underway and she was home for the next two weeks before they would return to Hawaii to continue filming.

It was a little cool on the Texas coast to film there, so they had moved the filming to Hawaii.

For this last song, she walked to the edge of the floor, staring into his eyes. Taking his hand, she pulled him up on stage and finished the song. Then she kissed him.

"And, now, Tucker Burnett and I are going to marry, but that's not part of the show. Merry Christmas and goodnight, everyone."

They stood staring at the camera waving.

"And that's a wrap," the director said. "Good job everyone."

She turned toward him and smiled.

The cameras and the mics all disappeared, leaving just them and the Christmas decorations on the stage they had created.

The preacher appeared in front of them and her sister was standing beside her along with her nieces. Travis and Tanner appeared at his side.

"Dearly beloved..." the preacher began.

Staring at her, he couldn't believe his luck. He couldn't believe the happiness she'd bestowed on him these last few months.

Getting hitched had not been on his life's plan, but now he was so grateful, and he intended on keeping her very happy.

As soon as the preacher told him he could kiss his bride, he pulled her into his arms and laid one on her that had the cameras flashing. He was claiming his wife right here in front of his family and he didn't care.

The smell of lavender filled the air.

"I'm so happy," Eugenia said as she wiped her eyes. "But where's Joshua?" she asked looking around.

Jacob started laughing. "He's on a booty call."

Eugenia gazed at Jacob, Joshua's brother. "What's a booty call?"

Aunt Rose cleared her throat. "Is there something you need, Eugenia?"

"Yes, I need to tell Joshua that he's next. Find that boy and tell him his days of being a hound dog are over. He's soon to be married."

Tucker grinned at his wife. "Mrs. Burnett, let's drink a toast to our life together."

"Uh, well, I had Emily order us non-alcoholic champagne. In eight, months our firstborn will arrive."

Tucker grinned and lifted Kendra in his arms. "You're an overachiever."

"No, my fired security man has potent sperm," she said. "We're going to have everything we wanted. A family of our own. A love that lasts forever."

Thank goodness he'd given in and ignored his own policies. Breaking that rule would give him a life filled with happiness.

And poor Joshua had no clue how his life was about to be turned upside down.

* * *

Available at Your Favorite Retailer

THANK YOU FOR READING TUCKER. This family has always been one of my favorites and I love bringing back Mama Eugenia as a ghost, still causing trouble, still matchmaking. Joshua, known for being the hound dog in the family, is next. Come see if Joshua is really a womanizer or if he's hiding a softer side.

* * *

Jennifer Moss is having a really bad day.... But it's about to get even worse...

"You won't be able to lay the book down! It keeps you wanting more until the very end... and then you still want more!" Sandy Sorola

Her teenage son's grades have plummeted. Her husband is distant

and cold, and now she's received a letter from the child she gave
up for adoption twenty-five years ago.
But a knock on the door, spins her world out of control.

Losing everything, she packs up and returns to Mustang Island
where the secrets from her past slowly unravel.

And the boy she left behind so many years ago helps her see that
this new beginning could be the best thing that's ever happened
to her.

**But will their secret child unravel their relationship before it
has a chance to begin again?**

*Lots of twists, turns, emotions, choices and so much more. Things that
happened long ago and make you look at something in a totally
different way.* Jennie F

Turn the Page for an excerpt from Secrets of a Summer Place

Excerpt From Secrets of a Summer Place

HOLLYWOOD, California

Staring at the envelope in her hand, Jennifer Moss sat in her Volvo waiting to pick up her son from the Hollywood high school baseball practice. Before she left the house, she'd grabbed the mail.

Now, an eerie sense of foreboding spiraled through her and filled her with anxiety. But then every time she received a piece of mail in which she didn't recognize the name on the envelope, her stomach churned.

Could this be from her? How many times had she gotten her hopes up for them only to be dashed? Would this be the same?

A soft breeze blew through the window on the cloudless day. For a moment, she stopped breathing as she stared at the address.

Madison Wilson, Austin, Texas.

Who did she know in Austin? Who was Madison Wilson? Anytime she received an envelope like this, her heart would pound in her chest and she would wonder if she'd been discovered.

Part of her wanted to be found, but then she would think of her life now. No one knew. It had been her secret for twenty-six years.

The memory of the house on Mustang Island overwhelmed her. She'd never returned after that summer, and since her parents' deaths, the house sat vacant. As much as she loved that place, she'd never go back because she would have to face the past.

A past that was heart wrenching and left her scared and hating her family.

Shouts from the field alerted her that the team would be leaving practice shortly. The coach always ended their practice with a pep rally. The kids were a good team and might make it to state this year. For her son's sake, she hoped so.

With a sigh, she tore open the envelope and pulled out the letter.

My name is Madison Wilson. According to the genealogy report, your DNA and my DNA are linked. It says you're my birth mother. I would like to speak to you and find out why you gave me up for adoption. I would also like to learn my medical background and even see if we have anything in common. If you are willing to speak to me, please contact me at...

A cry escaped her and the memories flooded her of that terrible day. Her name was Madison. Her heart leaped with a joy only a mother could feel.

Madison gave her address, her phone number, and even her email address.

It had taken twenty-five years, but her secret was about to be revealed. With a sigh, she stared out at the baseball field and let the memories of that day overwhelm her. How she had clung desperately to her child until her mother ripped the infant from her arms and gave her to the nurse.

She'd never seen the baby again after that day. Tears filled her eyes and trickled down her face. How many times had she thought of finding her and telling her how much she wanted to keep her? In the end, she thought it better not to disrupt her life and had done her best to move on. Now that child was grown and wondering why she had not been wanted.

But the opposite was true.

Oh, God, how she'd wanted to keep her. To love her and raise her as her own.

That time in her life had been the worst, and she'd never forgiven her mother for forcing her to give up her child for all the right reasons. They were not what Jennifer wanted to hear.

Sometimes doing the right thing was not the easiest. And having that child taken from her arms was gut-wrenching.

Her handsome son walked across the school yard, his head

down. Quickly she wiped the tears from her eyes and shoved the letter into her purse.

How was her family going to react to this news?

Her husband Ryan didn't know about her unwed pregnancy and subsequent birth. And her two smart, intelligent, beautiful children had no idea they had a half-sister. This secret had remained hidden for twenty-five years, but no more.

The door opened and her son slid in.

"Hi, Mom," he said and she could see he was upset.

"Bad day?" she asked.

"Kind of," he replied as he looked out the window of the car.

Something had been eating at him and she didn't know what. He refused to talk to her about it, and only said, *I'm okay*. But he wasn't. His grades had gone from honor roll to barely passing and she feared he was going to lose his scholarship to his favorite school.

No matter how she tried to approach him, the walls came slamming down. And today's mail would not make the situation any easier. Yet, she had waited so long for this letter. So long to hear from the baby she loved instantly.

He looked at her and studied her for a moment. "Are you all right?"

"Sure," she said, wondering how he could tell something was up. "Got something in my eye a moment ago."

"Oh," he said and gazed back out the window as she pulled out of the school parking lot.

"Is Dad going to be home tonight?"

"I don't know," she said. "This morning he left early because it's his surgery day."

Alex made a noise she couldn't quite interpret.

Her husband was a leading plastic surgeon in the Hollywood community and had worked on many stars in his practice. The money he brought in had made it easy for her to stay home and raise their two children.

But the hours he worked were sometimes long, and he often came home exhausted. Lately, he seemed to work longer and longer, though he'd promised her he was going to cut back his hours.

In the twenty years they'd been married, she often wondered if she'd traded love for money. Their marriage was good, but they spent so little time together, with him working so many hours. Sometimes it felt like they were two individual people living in the same house.

And there were days she felt lonely. If not for the kids, she would spend her evenings alone. And even they were growing up and moving on with their lives. Taylor would soon finish her second year of college, and next fall, Alex would be going to a university.

"How's the team doing?"

"If we continue to win, we should make the high school play-offs," he said, staring out the window.

Alex was normally so happy and excited and eager to talk, but in the last two months, he'd withdrawn into himself and she couldn't find a way to bring him out. The kid should be so excited about his team making the playoffs, and yet he didn't act like he cared.

Something was eating at her son and she missed the happy-go-lucky young man who was eager to begin his life.

"That's great news," she said. "When's your next game? Maybe me and your dad can both attend."

Ryan had only made it to one game. One, and soon their son's season and high school career would be at an end. Sometimes she hated Ryan's job, even though their life was luxurious because of his career.

That didn't excite Alex and she knew she had to learn what troubled him.

Sometimes she wished Ryan was an accountant or even a salesman and not a busy doctor.

Maybe after Alex graduated, she would get them reservations at Cozumel and take the kids down to the beach. She doubted that Ryan would take the time off. But it would be good to spend some time with her children.

The thought of Madison crossed her mind and she wondered if she would like to go with them.

"That would be nice," he said. "The next game is Saturday morning."

That was Ryan's tee time. Surely he could give up golfing one Saturday for his son. But nothing came between Ryan and his golf.

They pulled into the drive and the gate opened automatically. She pulled into the back garage. The pool man had been here today, and maybe later tonight, she'd get in the water and swim a few laps.

Closing the garage door, they both exited the car and walked into the house, entering through the laundry room.

"Good afternoon, Mrs. Moss, Alex," the maid said to her. "Dinner is in the oven. I'm leaving for the day."

"Thank you, Esmeralda," she said softly.

Alex walked past the woman and that was so unusual for him. Normally he would hug Esmeralda and tell her the cooking was divine. But not today.

Glancing at her son, Jennifer was worried. Maybe it was time to suggest counseling. Anything to keep his grades from falling even further. Anything to keep him from losing his scholarship. Anything to bring the boy she loved back to her.

"Good night," Esmeralda called as she exited the back door.

Jennifer walked into the massive kitchen and there was a salad sitting out and a casserole ready to turn on in the oven.

"Mom," Alex said, walking back into the kitchen. "Coach said I had to give you this."

She glanced at the envelope he held in his hand.

Taking it, she opened it to the letter inside.

"Damn it, Alex," she said as she read the letter. "What is going on?"

He shrugged. "Don't know."

"If you don't bring your grades up you're going to lose your scholarship. You're about to be kicked off the baseball team. This is not my son. Tell me what is wrong."

With a grimace, he turned and walked out of the kitchen. "Maybe I want to do high school over again. Maybe I'm a loser."

"Alex, don't walk away. Let's sit down and talk about this."

He ignored her and went up the stairs to his room.

Shaking her head, she couldn't wait for Ryan to get home. They had to have a serious talk with Alex, and she had to tell him she had another child. Madison.

Reaching inside the refrigerator, she pulled out a full bottle of wine and poured herself a glass.

It was going to be a hell of a night.

Chapter Two

Three hours later, Jennifer sat in the den, trying to watch a silly television show, her mind scattering from one child to the next. This evening, she tried to call Taylor, needing to hear the sound of her sweet voice. But she was a college kid and she must have been out with friends.

After calling her twice, she gave up.

She was so worried about Alex and couldn't wait to speak to Ryan about their son. It was time to consider getting professional help for him. Her star pupil's grades had reached bottom and his bubbly personality seemed to have died. What had happened to bring about this drastic change in him?

And no matter how hard she tried to reach him, she hit a wall.

Now there was Madison, and she didn't know how her husband and children were going to accept the news that she had given up a baby for adoption. After her mother took the baby from her arms, she'd done her best to try to keep the memory of her locked away. It was the only way she learned that she could keep the hurt from overwhelming her. And yet, not a day had gone by that she hadn't wondered about what she looked like and if she had a happy life.

Tonight, the house felt so empty and she feared what it would be like when Alex went to college. The place was like a tomb as she walked from room to room, pacing, worrying, thinking about the child she gave up and speculating when her husband would get home.

As she wandered through the house, she couldn't help but think how lonely it felt. Was this what her life would always be like? Her children in college, her husband at his job?

Tonight Ryan was later than ever. Normally, he walked in around eight at the very latest. Oftentimes, she'd wondered if he was really at the clinic or was he languishing in the arms of some woman. But then she would tell herself that she was being paranoid.

She had no reason to suspect her husband of cheating. None. His only mistress was his dedication to his profession. His patients.

Around seven, she gave up on him and cooked the casserole. Together, she and Alex sat at the table alone. The bright, bubbly boy of the past sat glumly and ate his dinner, seldom speaking. She'd tried to talk to him again about his grades, but it was like a wall had come down and she'd finally given up.

Did he want to fail?

Maybe when Ryan got home, he could reach their son. But Alex wasn't talking to her. Would he talk to his father?

Now sitting here in her favorite chair, the letter sat like a stone on her chest while the television rambled on, without her really seeing or hearing the noise.

What would this child look like? Would she have her hair and eye coloring or her father's? And where was her father? At twenty-five, her first daughter must be out of college. What had she done with her life?

Pain gripped Jennifer's chest at the thought of all she'd missed out on Madison's life. Her first steps, her first words, the cuddles and hugs. Her first dance recital, her first day of school.

Tears welled in her eyes and she got up and paced the floor.

Had her childhood been a great one? Did her adoptive parents give her the love she deserved? Would she hate Jennifer for giving her up?

While she knew her mother had been right to force her to give up the baby for adoption, it had been the hardest thing she'd ever done. And in her mind, she'd searched for some way to keep her. But being a mother at seventeen with no education would have guaranteed they would have struggled. Jennifer had been willing to make that sacrifice. She would have chosen the baby over her abundant life, but her mother had not given her that option.

And neither had Dylan, the boy she had loved and waited for day after day.

After her mother demanded that she give the child up, their relationship had never been the same. In many ways, Jennifer hated her mother and the way she had erased all the memories from that time from their family. It was like those nine months never happened, but they had.

There were no photos of Jennifer pregnant, nothing to show that time ever occurred. No photos of the baby. And yet a young life walked the earth because of Jennifer and Dylan. A young life that she never wanted to give up.

And the father of that child had been a huge disappointment. After the night of the party, they had spent every day together until her parents suspected her pregnancy and they left the island.

Early one morning, her parents packed up their summer home and returned to Dallas, leaving Jennifer's heart out near a sand dune. Though she'd called him multiple times, he'd never returned her calls or her letters.

Dylan's face appeared in her memory and she wondered what he looked like now. Was he happy? Had he ever thought of her again? But she would never know because she would not search him out. If he could walk away from her, then she didn't want to ever see him again.

Pacing the floor, she knew that life was about to change and she worried how her family would accept the news of her first daughter. No matter what they thought, she would welcome her child with open arms. So many years had passed since she'd seen her and she didn't want to waste any more time.

Tonight she would tell Ryan about Madison. Tonight everything would be revealed.

The doorbell rang. It was late. Who could be coming to see them at this time of night? She grabbed her phone and looked at the security app. Two policemen stood at the door.

Why were they here?

What if it was about Taylor? Could that be why she hadn't been able to reach her tonight?

She ran to the door, fear clutching her heart, feeling like she was in a dream. She could not face losing one of her children, ever. She'd lost one, she refused to lose another.

When she opened the door, they stared at her.

"Mrs. Moss?"

"Yes," she said, knowing instinctively from their expressions they were not delivering good news.

The man seemed to gather his courage as he took a deep breath. "We regret to inform you that your husband died of a heart attack this evening at his clinic."

"Ryan?" she said, a surreal feeling overcoming her. "Dr. Ryan Moss?"

"Yes, ma'am," the man said. "Do you have someone here with you?"

Ryan was dead. Her husband was dead.

"My son," she said. Oh my God, she would have to tell her children their father was dead.

"Alex," she cried, the slow realization that Ryan would never come home again hitting her as tears filled her eyes. No, their marriage had not been perfect, but still, she loved him.

Shock seemed to cushion her as the words reverberated through her mind. Ryan was dead. Her husband was dead.

All night, she'd been waiting for him to come home and he was dead. Dead. Ryan was dead.

Grief hit her like a tsunami wave knocking her to her knees. No more quick kisses in the morning. No more rushing out the door, barely acknowledging her. No more hugs in the night.

"Ma'am, are you all right?" the policeman asked.

No, she wasn't all right. Her world had exploded around her. Nothing would ever be the same after this day. The good news about Madison and the death of her husband were all delivered with a bang in one day.

"What's wrong, Mom," Alex said, coming up behind her. He pulled her up from the ground and gazed at the police officers.

"Your father died of a heart attack tonight," she said, throwing her arms around him and sobbing on his shoulder. "Ryan is dead."

Chapter Three

Jennifer sat in a chair on the front row of the graveside and gazed at the coffin. Her son sat on one side of her and her daughter on the other. Numb, she barely blinked while the preacher said his final words.

A cool breeze blew and the smell of the flowers piled on the casket and the many wreaths filled the air.

It was over. She was a widow. No more kisses. No more hugs.

No more long stares at her like he couldn't understand what she was saying, like his genius brain didn't accept the obvious.

Ryan never walked anywhere but ran. Now he was running in heaven and even probably doing surgery there. Someone must need a facelift in heaven.

All of his office staff attended the service, neighbors, his golfing friends, her ladies' club members, and even a few family members. They were all here, and yet as she stared at the coffin, she'd never felt more alone.

It didn't seem real.

Alex had not shed a single tear, but moved about woodenly like he feared at any moment he would break. Her daughter was taking her father's death especially hard and she gripped her hand in hers. Jennifer had cried until there were no tears left, but it still didn't feel real.

Any moment, she expected him to walk up and ask why everyone was so sad. *I'm right here. This has been a huge misunderstanding.*

But it was real. In the last two days, she'd had to deal with getting his body from the morgue to the funeral home. Contacting his family and telling them he was gone. His parents were deceased, but he had brothers and sisters, nieces and nephews, and many were sitting behind her.

Planning his funeral had been the most difficult thing she'd ever done. Not even her parents had been this hard. But how did you memorialize someone who was such a brilliant man? The church had been filled with well-known doctors who had operated with him or sent him patients.

The day felt surreal. But the sky was a dazzling blue and the California sun shone brightly on them.

They said the final prayer and she couldn't bow her head. All she could do was stare at the box that held his body. These were their final moments together and she sat trying to remember what he said to her that morning before he left. That final good-bye that neither one of them knew would be the end.

How could she know that would be the last time she'd see him?

The funeral director bent over to her. "Ma'am, the car is waiting for you whenever you're ready to leave. No hurry."

"Thank you," she heard herself say as she sat there wondering what was next.

Friends and family walked by and told her how sorry they were. And all she could do was nod and whisper *thank you*.

"Ma'am," Fiona Brown, his nurse from the office leaned down and took her hand, "I know this is a difficult time and I'm so sorry for your loss. We all loved Dr. Moss. But there are some things at the office that need to be taken care of right away. I'm sorry to tell you this, but the staff has not been paid in almost a month."

Jennifer jerked her head up and gazed at Fiona. "Really? Why not?"

Fiona shrugged. "I don't know, but some of them are starting to get really anxious about needing their pay."

What happened? Had Ryan known his employees were not being paid.

"Of course," she said, wondering why his bookkeeper had not paid his staff. "Give me just a few days and then I'll come in and take care of it."

She knew that the next few weeks were going to be so difficult straightening out their affairs. Changing everything from two people to one from their bank account to the mortgage, just everything.

After everyone had come by to pay their respects, she watched as people strolled off leaving her and the children alone.

Slowly they rose and walked to the casket still sitting on the rails. Staring down at the box that held his remains, she felt a chill race up her spine. This was it. Their final good-bye.

"I can't believe he's gone," her daughter said through her tears.

"Me either," Jennifer said. "Mourning him doesn't end today. The hardest part is yet to come."

She wrapped her arms around her children and they stared at the casket. Her son had been quiet for the last three days, saying very little. It almost seemed like he was angry and she didn't know how to reach him.

"Good-bye, Ryan," she said softly. "Rest in peace."

"Bye, Daddy," her daughter said.

Her son pulled away and walked toward the limo waiting for them.

"What's wrong with Alex," her daughter asked.

"I don't know," she said honestly. "Some people handle grief differently."

They turned and began to walk to the car. Her daughter said, "Last night, he got so angry with me when I asked him about Daddy."

Could something have happened between him and Ryan that was causing him to act out? After this weekend, when everything got back to a somewhat normal routine, she was going to ask him to see a counselor.

Tell the counselor what was eating him if he could not tell her. All she wanted was her cheerful son to return.

Somehow she had to reach him and help him get over whatever was troubling him. And now he had to deal with losing his father as well. It just didn't seem fair.

Her husband's employees were standing off to the side talking earnestly amongst themselves. One of the women gave a little laugh and shook her head.

They were just about to get into the limo. Alex stood holding the door open for them when Lily, her neighbor, and her son Kyle approached her.

"Jennifer, I just wanted to tell you how sorry I was about Dr.

Moss. He was such a great man and I just don't know how we're going to do without him."

Alex tensed and she could see him looking at Kyle. He mouthed the words *get her out of here.*

His face was red, and at any moment, she feared he was going to explode with fury. What was going on? Why was Alex acting this way?

"Come on, Mom, they need to go," Kyle said, taking her by the arm.

"If you need anything at all, please call me," Lily said. "I'm here for you."

"Thank you," Jennifer said.

Had Kyle and Alex gotten into a disagreement? They had been best of friends since they were in junior high. Come to think of it, she'd not seen Kyle at the house in ages.

Lily and Kyle walked away and Jennifer stood by the door of the limo and gazed at the people still at the cemetery. The office workers were still huddled together and she could tell they were frustrated.

Fiona rolled her eyes at Lily, and Jennifer couldn't help but think that was odd. She knew Lily was a patient because Ryan often made fun of the woman's requests. She'd had her boobs done twice, her nose, cheek implants, and even a tummy tuck.

He often called her plastic Barbie, but she kept coming in. The latest was a facelift.

But it was over. No one else would receive any help from Dr. Moss's hands. Now Jennifer had to go home, comfort her children, and start filing the necessary paperwork that dissolved everything they owned together.

"Come on, let's go home," she told Taylor and Alex. "Your father's family will be there and all that food that was sent in. Tomorrow it will be just the three of us. But today, we have family to entertain."

And she didn't feel like entertaining anyone.

"Mom, finals are next week. I need to go back to college day after tomorrow," Taylor said.

Jennifer felt her heart clench. She wasn't ready to part with her kids. Not yet. She needed them by her side.

"I understand," she said, softly knowing she had to let her go. They had to get on with their lives, but it seemed so quick. They had not had any time to adjust.

"Don't forget after finals, I'm going to London to study," she said. "Then I'll be home, but Daddy won't be here."

"No, he won't," Jennifer said. "Now we must learn to live without him."

Alex made a harrumph sound. Had he been angry at his father? Could that be what was troubling him? And what did Kyle have to do with the rage that seemed to be seeping from Alex?

Want more...Available at your favorite retailer!

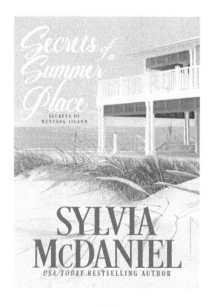

Contemporary Romance
Burnett Brides Contemporary Times
Travis

Tanner

Tucker

Joshua

Jacob

Return to Cupid, Texas
Cupid Stupid

Cupid Scores

Cupid's Dance

Cupid Help Me!

Cupid Cures

**Cupid's Heart

Cupid Santa

**Cupid Second Chance

Cupid Charmer

Cupid Crazy

Cupid's Bachelorette

Return to Cupid Box Set Books 1-3

Cupid Help Me Box Set Books 4-6

**The Unlucky Bride

Contemporary Romance
My Sister's Boyfriend

The Wanted Bride

The Reluctant Santa

The Relationship Coach

Secrets, Lies, & Online Dating

Bride, Texas Multi-Author Series
**The Unlucky Bride

ALSO BY

Lipstick and Lead 2.0
Nailing the Hit Man
Nailing the Billionaire
Nailing the Single Dad

Secrets of Mustang Island
Secrets of a Summer Place
Secrets of a Runaway Bride
Secrets From the Past

The Langley Legacy
Collin's Challenge

Short Sexy Reads
Racy Reunions Series
Paying For the Past
Her Christmas Lie
Cupid's Revenge

Western Historicals
A Hero's Heart
Second Chance Cowboy
Ethan

American Brides
**Katie: Bride of Virginia

Angel Creek Christmas Brides
Charity
Ginger
Minnie
Cora

The Burnett Brides Series

The Rancher Takes A Bride
The Outlaw Takes A Bride
The Marshal Takes A Bride
The Christmas Bride
Boxed Set

Lipstick and Lead Series
Desperate
Deadly
Dangerous
Daring
**Determined
Deceived
Defiant
Devious
Lipstick and Lead Box Set Books 1-4
**Quinlan's Quest

Mail Order Bride Tales
**A Brother's Betrayal
**Pearl
**Ace's Bride

Scandalous Suffragettes of the West
**Abigail
Bella
Mistletoe Scandal

Southern Historical Romance
A Scarlet Bride
Charity

The Cuvier Women
Wronged

Betrayed
Beguiled
Boxed Set

** **Denotes a sweet book.**

Want to learn about my new releases before anyone else? Sign up for my New Book Alert and receive a free book.

USA Today Best-selling author, Sylvia McDaniel obviously has too much time on her hands. With over eighty western historical and contemporary romance novels, she spends most days torturing her characters. Bad boys deserve punishment and even good girls get into trouble. Always looking for the next plot twist, she's known for her sweet, funny, family-oriented romances.

Married to her best friend for over twenty-five years, they recently moved to the state of Colorado where they like to hike, and enjoy the beauty of the forest behind their home with their spoiled dachshunds Zeus and Bailey. (Zeus has his own column in her newsletter.)

Their grown son, still lives in Texas. An avid football watcher, she loves the Broncos and the Cowboys, especially when they're winning.

www.SylviaMcDaniel.com
Sylvia@SylviaMcDaniel.com
The End!

Printed in the USA
CPSIA information can be obtained
at www.ICGtesting.com
LVHW020208050124
767940LV00059B/888